Governess Perdita Frayne was determined to give satisfaction in her new post, in spite of her unsuitable youth and prettiness. She tried to obey the order to keep her young charges away from the notorious Jason Hawkesworth – though the reason was a mystery to her.

But accidental meetings did occur . . . Perdita was drawn to Jason's rakish good looks, but outraged by his arrogance. He mocked at the "Prim Miss Frayne", but kissed the lovely, headstrong Perdita. What could she think of a man who humiliated her, yet offered her his protection?

At the same time, sinister and frightening 'accidents' happened at Tarrington Chase, and Jason was accused. But Perdita had her own theories about this. As her attraction to Jason grew, she was drawn deeper into danger.

Sylvia Thorpe

Tarrington Chase

CORGI BOOKS
A DIVISION OF TRANSWORLD PUBLISHERS LTD

TARRINGTON CHASE
A CORGI BOOK 0 552 10615 1

Originally published in Great Britain by
Hutchinson and Co. Ltd. under the title Dark Heritage.

PRINTING HISTORY
Hutchinson edition published 1968
Corgi edition published 1977

This book is set in 10/12½pt Times.

Corgi Books are published by Transworld Publishers Ltd.,
Century House, 61–63 Uxbridge Road,
Ealing, London, W.5.
Made and printed in Great Britain by
Hunt Barnard Printing Ltd., Aylesbury, Bucks.

I

A gig driven by a groom had been sent to meet the new governess at the little market town where she had alighted from the stage-coach, and now with each passing mile Perdita Frayne's spirits sank lower. She was a stranger to the Welsh Marches, and had not expected Tarrington Chase to be so isolated, or in surroundings of such rugged grandeur. Accustomed only to the neat and undramatic countryside around London, she had been unprepared for this land of endless hills through which the road wound its laborious way; these towering, wooded slopes with, here and there, outcrops of bare rock rearing above the trees. Among the hills the Wye coiled and twisted like some fantastic serpent, at one moment rippling over shallows, and the next flowing dark and deep and silent, while the blue distance glimpsed now and then as they climbed some ridge was filled with yet more tree-clad heights which the groom told her was the Royal Forest of Dean. Even the gentler aspects of the countryside, the apple orchards with boughs already bending beneath the weight of ripening fruit, and the lush meadows where white-faced cattle grazed, seemed to Perdita to be dominated by the secret, brooding presence of the hills.

For some time they had been descending a steep slope where the road was enclosed in a tunnel of trees, but as they reached the bottom it emerged suddenly into the open and swung to the right along the foot of the hill, with level meadows on its farther side. The groom pointed across the fields, and upwards, and said laconically:

"There'er be, miss! Tarrington Chase!"

Perdita followed the direction of the pointing hand. Beyond the meadows, the swift-flowing river swept like a moat along the foot of wooded slopes steeper, even, than the hill they had just descended, and on the highest crest could be glimpsed a great house. Poised there against the sky, full in sunlight yet backed by an ominous curtain of purple-black storm clouds, it seemed at once to beckon and to repel, like the setting of some old legend. Perdita, trying to subdue a wave of misgiving sharper than any which had preceded it, said in a voice which, try as she might, still betrayed something of the dismay she felt:

"How in the world do we reach the house? Surely there is no road up that hillside?"

"Not on this side, miss! We do go round through the village, look! Another two or three mile."

He whipped the horse to a smarter pace, for the clouds were sweeping irresistibly across the sky, blotting out the sunlight and seeming to rest on the summits of the hills, while a growl of thunder sounded faintly in the distance. Perdita looked anxiously about her in the vain hope of discovering some shelter from the imminent downpour, for the open carriage offered no protection, and the prospect of arriving drenched and bedraggled to face her new employer was a daunting one.

Ahead of them the road swung away from the river and began to climb again, bordered now by a stone wall on the left. Straight ahead, a crumbling gateway in the wall led to a lesser track which wound through parkland dotted with clumps of trees, and though work had recently begun on repairing the gateway, the entrance still stood open. The groom drew rein, hesitated for a moment, and then with another glance at the darkening sky urged the horse briskly through the gap. Perdita, glancing at him, read uneasiness in his face and felt an illogical twinge of alarm.

They were very close to the river now, and, beyond it, the precipitous slopes of Tarrington Chase hung above them, as dark as the storm clouds and as threatening, the broad stream flowing, swift and sinister, in the shadow of the trees which clothed the hillside to its very brink. In the stillness preceding the storm the whole world seemed to be waiting, and Perdita found herself waiting, too, dreading she knew not what.

Then she heard the swift drumming of approaching hooves, and a rider burst into view around a clump of trees on their right, plunging recklessly down the slope to bring his mount rearing to a halt across the track in front of the gig. The groom cursed, more in dismay than anger, and Perdita uttered a faint cry as their own horse, startled by that abrupt arrival, whinnied and tried to shy.

The big roan pranced forward, and was reined in again alongside the gig. Its rider said in a voice of concentrated fury: "What the devil are you doing on my land? Get back the way you came, and be thankful you have a woman with you, or you would not escape so lightly!"

"Mr 'Awkesworth, sir!" The groom, with difficulty controlling his nervous horse, spoke in a tone at once protesting and placating. "There be a storm coming up, look, and us must reach the village afore 'er do break. For the young lady's sake, sir!"

The horseman glanced indifferently at Perdita. He was a big man, lean yet powerful, with black hair and a harsh, dark, aquiline face. The sort of face, she thought suddenly, that one might imagine a pirate or a brigand to have. Beneath thick, black brows, his deep-set eyes were of a brown so light that it was almost yellow. They studied her critically from head to foot, flashed for a second to the battered trunk behind her, and then returned to her face. The hard mouth curved a fraction, contemptuously.

"The new governess, no doubt!" he said sardonically. "You are a brave woman, ma'am, to enter the employment of the witch of Tarrington!"

She was too astonished to reply. For a second or two longer Mr Hawkesworth continued to regard her, and then turned his attention once more to the groom.

"As for you, my man, you should know me better than to suppose I do not mean what I say! The days when the whole village might come traipsing across this land ended when I became the master of Mays Court, and the sooner you all accept that fact, the better!"

The groom began to protest again, but was cut peremptorily short. "Had you kept to the road, you could easily have reached Cleeve Farm before the storm breaks. If you are really concerned for this young woman, you will still endeavour to do so."

He reined the roan back, and the groom, muttering under his breath but obviously resigned to defeat, turned the gig and then whipped the horse to a pace which caused the light vehicle to jolt and sway alarmingly over the uneven track. Perdita clutched at the side to steady herself, but could not refrain from looking back to see what had become of the extraordinary Mr Hawkesworth.

He still sat his horse on the slope below the trees, a dark, forbidding figure in the forbidding landscape. High above, over the crest of Tarrington Chase, lightning ripped the pall of cloud, and Perdita flinched as, for a fraction of a second, the whole scene was bathed in dazzling radiance. When she looked again, horse and rider had gone.

"What a disagreeable man!" she said indignantly. "What harm, pray, were we doing by driving along this track?"

"B'aint a question o' harm, miss!" the groom replied bitterly. "Colonel Travers, as owned Mays Court till a year ago, were a proper gentleman, and let folk use the short cut as much as they liked, but Jason 'Awkesworth be a different matter! This land do be his now, look, and him won't let no one forget it. That's ever the way o' them as had naught to start with!"

Perdita felt slightly puzzled by this. Mr Hawkesworth's appearance indicated that he was a man of
wealth and fashion, his speech betokened a person of
education. She would not have supposed him to be a
parvenu.

"And for the likes o' him to speak so impudent of
her ladyship!" the groom continued aggrievedly. "I tell
you, miss, 'twere a bad day for Tarrington when Jason
'Awkesworth bought Mays Court! Him, with his
fancy-pieces and his heathen blackamoor! Pity him
didn't stay in foreign parts!"

There was enough in these words to increase Perdita's already lively curiosity, but she felt that it would
not do to begin her sojourn at Tarrington Chase by
gossiping with the servants, so she returned a non-
committal reply. No doubt, since Hawkesworth was
obviously the bête-noir of the village, she would learn
more about him in due course. For good or ill, he was
clearly not a man who could be ignored, and it occurred to her that his name, at least, was curiously apt.
There was something decidedly hawk-like about that
dark, predatory face and fierce golden eyes.

The storm was now very close, and as the gig bowled
through the gateway and slowed to climb the hill, the
first big spots of rain came pattering down. By the time
Cleeve Farm was reached it was raining heavily, but
the farmer's wife made Perdita welcome, ushering her
into a musty parlour and carrying her bonnet and pelisse off to the kitchen to dry them by the fire. Like
Jason Hawkesworth, she appeared to know without
being told that Perdita was the new governess, but as
Perdita herself had been born and reared in a country
village, this neither surprised nor dismayed her. In any

small and close-knit community, the arrival of a
stranger was bound to arouse curiosity.

She wished, though, that the woman's sense of what
was proper had not compelled her guest to sit solitary
in the parlour, for this gave her time to think, and to
wonder uneasily what kind of reception awaited her at
Tarrington Chase. She had not yet met her employer.
An advertisement in the *Morning Post* had led to an
interview in London with an elderly lawyer, as a result
of which she had found herself engaged by Lady Tarrington to take charge of her ladyship's fourteen-year-
old grand-daughter, Melissa. Perdita did not doubt her
ability to carry out her duties, and she had made no
secret of the fact that she was only twenty-one, but in-
terviews with other prospective employers had taught
her that such ladies usually preferred a governess who
was no longer young, and certainly one who was not
well-favoured.

There was a dim and spotty mirror hanging on the
parlour wall, and Perdita walked across to it and stood
staring critically at her reflection, trying to see herself
through Lady Tarrington's eyes. This brought little reassurance. Thick, dark-brown hair which, no matter
how primly it was dressed, never failed to revert to its
natural waves and curls; clear, pale skin, and a mouth
too warmly curved for severity; eyes more green than
grey, set slightly aslant above high cheek-bones—cat's
eyes, her brother Peter used to call them when he
wanted to tease her. Perdita did not consider herself
beautiful, or even pretty, and had been as much astonished as dismayed the first time it was made plain to
her that men found her attractive. Power to attract the
opposite sex was no advantage, in that year of 1812, to

a solitary young woman obliged to earn her own living, since it was in the highest degree unlikely that it would lead to marriage. It was, in fact, a handicap, for families requiring a governess frequently included elder sons of impressionable age, and Perdita's efforts to find suitable employment had met with no success until she applied for the post at Tarrington Chase. Even now, she often wondered uneasily whether her success then was due simply to the fact that Lady Tarrington had been unable to interview her in person, and she had been only partly reassured to learn from the lawyer that her ladyship's only other grandchild was a boy of nine.

So it was with considerable trepidation that she presently resumed her journey. The rain had ceased, but the sky still looked angry, and the groom gave it as his opinion that the storm would return before nightfall, a prophecy which did nothing to raise Perdita's spirits. She was not afraid of thunderstorms, but, watching the one which had just passed, seeing the whole valley blotted out by a hissing curtain of rain while the thunder crashed and rolled among the hills, she had felt that its violence was disturbingly at one with the wildness of the country, and with the turbulent undercurrents which already she sensed stirring beneath the surface.

The road still skirted the wall bounding the park of Mays Court, and presently they passed a pair of tall, wrought-iron gates leading to an avenue of elms, though the house itself was not visible. Half a mile farther on lay the village of Tarrington, a picturesque huddle of cottages, a black-and-white-timbered inn

and a church with a square tower, all clustered about
the old stone bridge which spanned the river.

Beyond the river the road began to climb once more,
slanting across the shoulder of the hill, which on this
side was not wooded, but clad in a mantle of bracken
which at times reached as high as the horse's withers.
Outcrops of rock shouldered their way through the undergrowth, and huge boulders hung poised, looking
as though the merest touch would send them bounding
down into the valley. Harebells nodded among the
bracken stems, blackberries were beginning to ripen,
and the gorse thickets were still sprinkled with golden
blossoms.

Halfway up the hill, the road turned sharply in a
hairpin bend and began to go back on its course at a
higher level, until from a peak where the bracken gave
way to springy grass Perdita could see the village far
below, like a child's toy among the green meadows. At
last the ground levelled out, and she realised that here
on the summit of Tarrington Chase there was a stretch
of comparatively flat, undulating land of far greater extent than could be guessed from the valley. The road
dipped and rose and dipped again, and then before
them was an imposing gateway, its pillars crowned by
griffons with outspread wings.

Beyond the gate, and the lodge which guarded it,
they passed again into the shadow of trees, and another
half-mile of rolling parkland brought them to the
house itself, a great, rambling mansion composed of a
medley of architectural styles. From the main entrance,
with the Tarrington arms carved in stone above it, Perdita was conducted through a Great Hall of enormous

proportions, up a fine, seventeenth-century staircase, and eventually into a pleasant sitting-room with windows commanding a magnificent view over the valley. Here her new employer was waiting to receive her.

Perdita's first impression of Lady Tarrington was of one of the most unprepossessing women she had ever seen, an impression which further acquaintance with her was to do nothing to alter. Her fashionably dressed but rather sparse white hair framed a face which was thin and forbidding and absolutely colourless—skin like parchment, light brows and lashes, pale lips, and eyes as grey and cold as ice. The nose was long, somewhat pinched about the nostrils, and the mouth set in a bitter, down-curving line.

The sharp, cold gaze passed over Perdita in one swift, comprehensive survey which took in the neat but shabby pelisse, the carefully darned gloves and unfashionable bonnet, and noted also the grace of the tall slender figure and the youthful charm of the face beneath the bonnet's brim. Hostility gathered in the pale eyes, the hostility of a plain and bitter old woman towards a young and attractive one. Lady Tarrington frowned, and said curtly:

"You look a great deal younger than I expected!"

"I am turned twenty-one, my lady," Perdita replied meekly, "and I have had charge of four young ladies for the past three years."

"Yes, yes, so I have been informed!" her ladyship said impatiently. "Your qualifications for the post are, I admit, adequate, but qualifications, Miss Frayne, are not the only consideration. I know very little of your family background. Your father, I understand, was in Holy Orders?"

"He was the vicar of Tillesden, in Middlesex, for the last twenty years of his life, ma'am. He died three years ago. My mother predeceased him by four years."

"Have you no brothers or sisters?"

"I had one brother, ma'am, who was three years older than I. He was a midshipman under Lord Nelson, and was killed at Trafalgar."

Lady Tarrington picked up a letter from the small table beside her, and consulted it. "Since your father's death you have lived with relations in London," she remarked. "Why have you left their protection?"

Perdita hesitated, for how could she tell this forbidding old lady the truth? After her father's death, she had been overcome with gratitude when Hannah Mulstead, a distant cousin whom she had met only once, offered her a home; even when she found that she was expected to take charge of Mrs Mulstead's four tiresome daughters, she had done so willingly. As time went by she realised that Hannah's only motive in taking her in was to acquire a governess without the necessity of paying wages, but she might have been resigned to staying there had it not been for Hannah's husband, Henry, and his constant, furtive pursuit of her, Henry, fat and pale, becoming steadily bolder, more difficult to evade—no, she could never tell Lady Tarrington that.

"I had always lived in the country, ma'am," she said at length, "and could not accustom myself to London. Besides, I did not like being made to feel that I was living upon charity."

Lady Tarrington made no response to this. "You are aware, of course," she said, "that you are required to take complete charge of my grand-daughter, Miss Me-

lissa Tarrington. There is also my grandson, the present
baronet, who is almost ten years old. His education is
in the hands of his tutor, but when he is not at his lessons he, too, will be in your care."

Perdita said meekly that she had been informed of
this. The information that her prospective charges, like
herself, had lost both parents had immediately aroused
her sympathy, a feeling greatly increased now that she
had met their grandmother. One could not imagine
Lady Tarrington showing much affection to anyone.

Her ladyship had laid the letter down again and was
tapping it with thin, jewelled fingers. After a minute
or so of silence she said abruptly:

"In the ordinary way, Miss Frayne, I would not
dream of engaging anyone as young as yourself, and
that I have done so now is simply in the nature of an
experiment. My grand-daughter's previous governess,
Miss Caterby, who died a month ago, was an excellent
creature, but she had been governess also to Melissa's
mama, and was very advanced in years. Melissa has
few friends, for there are no young ladies of good family living within easy reach, and it occurred to me that
now that she is growing up, the constant companionship of a young woman might be beneficial to her. I repeat, however, that this is merely an experiment. At the
end of three months, I will decide whether or not it has
been a successful one."

Perdita stood with meekly lowered gaze, trying to
hide her dismay, and her indignation that the position
had not been made clear to her at the outset. In accepting the post at Tarrington Chase she had burned
her bridges behind her, for Hannah Mulstead had made
it very plain that, having chosen to leave, Perdita would

not be expected to return, so if her employment with
Lady Tarrington lasted no longer than three months,
she would find herself in a difficult situation indeed.
She could only hope that she and her new pupil would
take to each other, and resolved to do her utmost to
make the experiment a success.

Lady Tarrington summoned a servant and sent him
to the schoolroom with a message that the children
were to come and make the acquaintance of their new
governess. While they waited, she said coldly:

"Your arrival, Miss Frayne, was somewhat later
than I expected, but no doubt you were obliged to wait
in the village for the duration of the storm?"

"We sheltered at a farm, my lady," Perdita explained. "Cleeve Farm, I think it was called."

The old lady's brows lifted. "Indeed? I would have
supposed you to have passed Cleeve Farm before the
storm broke."

"I think we might have done, ma'am, but the groom
you sent to meet me attempted to take a short cut
through a private park, and a gentleman whom I take
to be the owner of the property stopped us and compelled us to turn back."

Perdita had expected this to provoke some annoyance on Lady Tarrington's part, but she was taken
aback by the sheer fury which blazed into the old lady's
eyes and twisted her thin lips.

"That man!" She almost spat the words, making
them sound as vicious as a curse. "There is no end to
his insolence, his ill-bred effrontery! He insults me in
every conceivable way!" She was silent for a moment,
her hands gripping the arms of her chair like jewelled
claws as she struggled to control her anger. After a lit-

2

tle she continued more calmly: "This is a matter, Miss
Frayne, of which I intended to speak to you later, but
since you have already had the misfortune to encounter
Jason Hawkesworth, I will speak now. That man must
never, at any time or under any circumstances, have
anything to do with either of my grandchildren. To
disregard that order will mean instant dismissal. Do
you understand me?"

"Perfectly, my lady," Perdita assured her hurriedly,
wondering as she spoke what lay behind the command,
and what caused the hatred—for it was nothing less—
which mere mention of Hawkesworth had aroused. It
was an emotion he seemed to provoke in all quarters.

The door opened, and a young girl in a white muslin
dress with a blue sash came into the room. After a
fleeting glance at Perdita she addressed her ladyship.

"Stephen is with Edward, Grandmama. I have sent
for him."

Lady Tarrington nodded. "Very well, Melissa. This
is your new governess, Miss Frayne."

Perdita smiled and held out her hand. "I am happy
to make your acquaintance, Miss Tarrington."

Melissa touched the outstretched hand with limp,
cool fingers, but did not return the smile. She was tall
for her age and rather thin, with a long, slender neck
and a quantity of very fine, light-brown hair. Not a
pretty girl, for her cast of countenance was much like
her grandmother's, with the same light-grey eyes, and a
discontented look about the mouth. Perdita's heart
sank, but she reminded herself that it was wrong to be
too greatly swayed by first impressions.

Footsteps sounded outside, a man's voice made some
indistinguishable remark and was answered in childish

tones. A small boy in nankeen trousers and a frilled shirt came in, followed by a young man, and ran across to Lady Tarrington with all the confidence of one certain of a warm welcome. For the first time her ladyship's expression softened.

"Stephen, my dear," she said kindly, "I have sent for you so that you may meet your new governess. Miss Frayne, this is my grandson, Sir Stephen Tarrington."

The youthful baronet turned, looking at Perdita with curiosity and a certain wariness, and she was stabbed by a sharp sense of shock. Like his sister, Stephen was slim and brown-haired, but his eyes were a remarkable golden colour such as she had never seen before that day. Exactly the same colour as the eyes which, a little while earlier, had looked at her from Jason Hawkesworth's dark, ruthless face.

II

Stephen made a little bow, quaint in its formality, but continued to regard Perdita with a hint of perplexity. "You do not look like a governess, ma'am," he said frankly. "I thought you would be a very old lady, like Miss Caterby."

She was amused, but tried not to show it, remembering how humiliating the laughter of adults could be when one was very young. He was, she decided, a far more attractive child than his sister, and though rather thin and small for his age, with a look of delicacy about him, had a lively, mischievous expression which was more taking than Melissa's indifference.

"I am sorry if that disappoints you, Sir Stephen," she

said gravely. "I shall, of course, grow old one day, but not, I believe, until *you* have outgrown my care."

He looked rather uncertain, and then a brilliant smile irradiated his small face. "I'm not disappointed, ma'am, I'm glad," he informed her. "You are much prettier than Miss Caterby."

"It is impolite, Stephen, to make personal remarks of that nature," Lady Tarrington put it, but the rebuke lacked force and Perdita guessed that Stephen could do little wrong in his grandmother's eyes. "Miss Frayne will think that you have no notion how to behave."

"She will, indeed!" remarked the young man who had accompanied Stephen into the room. "I trust, ma'am, that you will not suppose him to have learned such shamelessness from me."

Perdita glanced doubtfully at Lady Tarrington, who said in an expressionless voice: "Miss Frayne, allow me to make known to you Mr Eastly, my grandson's tutor."

Perdita with difficulty suppressed a gasp, for Mr Eastly had an air of fashion which one would certainly not expect to find in a mere tutor, and she had taken him to be a member of the family. He looked to be only a few years older than herself, and was of medium height, fair-haired and blue-eyed, with a countenance which was pleasing without being precisely handsome. There was nothing extravagant about his clothes, but they were of a cut and quality which could never have come from a country tailor, while his easy manner was not that of a dependent. She found that he was regarding her with an appreciation as great, even though not as frankly expressed, as Stephen's, and bestowed a

frosty glance upon him as she acknowledged the intro-
duction.

"Children, take Miss Frayne to see your apartments,
and her own," Lady Tarrington commanded. "Her
trunk will have been carried up by now. Miss Frayne,
we will talk again later. There are a number of matters
I wish to discuss with you. Edward, be good enough to
remain with me for a few minutes."

Obediently Stephen and Melissa led the way from
the room, and as Perdita followed them she reflected
that either Lady Tarrington was an eccentric, or this
was a very odd household indeed. She had never before
heard of a tutor who dressed like a man of fashion, or
whose employer called him by his Christian name.

The children's quarters, to which they led her by
way of a bewildering succession of corridors, staircases
and intervening rooms, were in the oldest part of the
house, a two-storied wing, built of stone and shrouded
in ivy, which appeared to jut out from the sprawling
mass of the main building. Their rooms were all on the
upper floor, the lower being occupied, as Melissa
grudgingly informed Perdita, by the armoury, the
agent's office, and the muniment room where the estate and family records were kept.

A corridor ran the length of the schoolroom floor,
terminating in a spiral staircase which led down to a
door opening on to the gardens. On one side of the
corridor was the schoolroom and, beyond it, the apartment which would now be Perdita's, while opposite to
these were three smaller rooms which led into one another. That nearest to the spiral stair was Stephen's,
Melissa's was at the other end, and the room between,
where Nurse had once slept, was now unoccupied.

Having imparted this information, and ushered Perdita into her own room, Melissa said that she and Stephen would wait in the schoolroom until Miss Frayne was ready to join them. Stephen showed an inclination to linger, but his sister took him firmly by the hand and led him out, closing the door behind them with an air of finality.

Perdita looked about her. The room was moderately large, but could scarcely have been described as a comfortable apartment. The floor, covered with rush matting, was of stone, and though at some period of its history the walls had been oak-panelled from floor to ceiling, this panelling was now black with age, while the furnishings, a motley collection of pieces of varying degrees of antiquity, appeared to have been banished to their present surroundings when they became too shabby or too outmoded for the principal part of the house. The mullioned window was set rather high, and the view from it even further restricted by the massive thickness of the walls and the crowding ivy, so that little could be seen but the branches of some nearby trees. Perdita sighed, and began rather dispiritedly to unpack her few belongings.

When she had arranged everything to her satisfaction, and made herself tidy, she went to the schoolroom, determined to get to know her charges better. Melissa was sitting at the table, turning the pages of a book, while Stephen, prone on the hearthrug, played with a little, golden-coloured spaniel. When Perdita entered, the puppy came frisking to greet her, and she bent to fondle it.

"What a dear little creature!" she exclaimed. "How fortunate you are to have so delightful a pet!"

"It belongs to Stephen," Melissa said without looking up. "I do not care for dogs."

"Do you like them, Miss Frayne?" Stephen asked anxiously as he scrambled to his feet.

"Indeed I do!" Perdita picked up the puppy, laughing as it nuzzled eagerly at her cheek. "When my parents were alive, we were never without one."

She was rewarded by Stephen's wide, enchanting smile. "His name is Russet," he informed her, "and he is quite well-behaved, whatever Melissa may say. Of course, he is still very young, but I am training him, and he learns extremely fast."

"I am sure he does," Perdita agreed with a smile. She put Russet into his arms and watched him hug the little animal, pressing his cheek against the top of its silky head. It was not difficult to see that he adored his pet, and she was to find later that he kept the dog with him on every possible occasion, only submitting with the utmost reluctance to his grandmother's decree that at night it must be banished to a kennel among the outbuildings.

Perdita's reaction to Russet's presence in the schoolroom set the seal on Stephen's approval of the new governess, and since he was a friendly child, wholly without shyness, he was prepared to chatter away as much as she would permit. Perdita was glad of it, and wished that his sister would show even a trifle of the same willingness to accept her. Melissa was perfectly civil, but no more responsive than she had been in her grandmother's presence, and once or twice Perdita thought she saw resentment in the girl's eyes.

Supper was brought to them by a maidservant whom the children addressed as "Gwenny", a dark young woman of about Perdita's age, with a pretty, sharp-featured face. She stared curiously at Perdita, but told her, civilly enough, that it was her duty to look after the schoolroom wing, and perhaps Miss would give her any instructions she thought necessary. At least, Perdita thought with relief, the maid seemed friendly enough.

When the meal was over, Melissa announced that it was customary at this hour for her and her brother to spend some time in the drawing-room with their grandmother before going to bed, and that Miss Caterby had always accompanied them. The information was given in a faintly challenging tone, as though some argument were expected, but Perdita merely said calmly:

"Then if that is the custom, Miss Tarrington, let us go at once, for it will not do to keep her ladyship waiting. You will have to tell me such things, you know, just as you will have to show me the way, for it will take a little while for me to learn my way about."

"I will show you the way, Miss Frayne," Stephen said promptly. "We'll go through the Long Gallery. That will be quickest."

The Long Gallery, a beautiful room of the Tudor period, with tall windows all along one side, and two magnificently carved fireplaces on the other, faced west, and was flooded with evening light. Perdita looked about her with admiration, and then, near the door at the far end, a portrait caught her attention. Involuntarily she paused, staring at the haughty gentleman who looked back at her from the canvas; a gentleman in the ruffled and beribboned dress of the Restoration Court, with aquiline features and deep-set, gold-brown eyes.

"That is another Stephen Tarrington," the little boy's voice said beside her. "He was the first baronet."

With difficulty Perdita withdrew her gaze from the compelling painted countenance, and smiled down at the speaker. "Were you named after him?"

"I suppose I was," he replied reflectively. "The eldest son is always called Stephen, as Papa and I were, or Humphrey, like Grandpapa."

"Stephen, Grandmama is waiting for us," Melissa said sharply. "Do not dawdle here!"

In the drawing-room, Lady Tarrington sat talking to Edward Eastly, but it was plain that the tutor had not been summoned there as a dependent merely to discuss the progress of his pupil. To Perdita's astonishment he wore evening dress, and appeared so much at his ease that she realised it must be usual for him to dine with her ladyship. He rose to greet the newcomers, and after a few civilities had been exchanged engaged the children in a game of lottery tickets at one end of the room, while at the other, Lady Tarrington proceeded to subject Perdita to a rigorous cross-examination, and to give her a great many instructions regarding her charges. Perdita answered the questions patiently and listened attentively to the commands, though she could not help noticing that these were concerned far more with Stephen than with his sister.

Only towards the end of the interview was she guilty of allowing her attention to wander, and that was because she had discovered, hanging above the fireplace, yet another portrait with eyes of that curious tawny colour. It was the likeness of a fair-haired young man, and from the style of dress had apparently been painted some fifteen years earlier.

"That is a portrait of my son, Miss Frayne!" Lady Tarrington's cold voice broke in upon her thoughts. "No doubt you are remarking the resemblance between us."

Perdita agreed politely that she was, and in fact there was a certain similarity of feature, though the face in the portrait was far more amiable than the old lady's forbidding countenance. Once again a puzzled question formed in her mind, as she remembered yet another face, dark and strong and totally unlike the pictured one, yet with those same golden eyes.

Next morning, alone with Melissa in the school-room—for Stephen had his lessons in the library—Perdita sought again to establish some sort of contact with her pupil, but without success. Melissa was polite and obedient, performing every task required of her and meekly accepting correction when it was needful, but she remained completely unapproachable. Perdita tried to tell herself that it was merely a question of time, but could not entirely conquer a feeling of inadequacy.

In the afternoon she took both children for a walk, for that had been one of Lady Tarrington's instructions, but she was disconcerted to find Mr Eastly joining them. Melissa and Stephen welcomed him with delight, and Perdita could find no reason to refuse his courteous request to accompany them. She did not even know why she felt she ought to do so, except that he seemed so much like one of the family that she could not rid herself of a nagging sense of impropriety.

The gardens of Tarrington Chase were extensive, and laid out with an artist's eye for the magnificent views on every side. Avenues and walks and shrubberies all offered cunningly placed points of vantage,

and Perdita was constantly being surprised by some
new and splendid vista opening before her. From several places she could see the road she had traversed the
previous day, the farm where they had sheltered, and a
large, handsome house amid gardens and parkland
which she assumed was Mays Court, though she
thought it prudent not to ask if this were so.

After a while, she was astonished to see the river,
which she had imagined to be to the left of where they
stood, far below them on the right, but Edward, seeing
her surprise, explained that it flowed in a great loop
around the base of the hill; a loop some five miles long
yet less than a mile across at its neck.

"In ancient times the river was an important line of
defence," he continued, "for it means that the summit
of the hill can only be reached with any ease from the
south-west, where the village now stands. This has
been a stronghold since before history began, and parts
of the present house—the schoolroom wing, for example—date from the fourteenth century, though the
Tarringtons did not acquire the estate until 1570. Since
then, however, it has passed in unbroken succession
from father to son."

"Not all the time," Stephen contradicted. "*I* inherit-
ed from Grandpapa."

"Yes, you did," Edward agreed calmly, "and no
doubt Miss Frayne is impressed by that singularity.
Whether she is equally impressed by your manners is
open to doubt."

Stephen coloured furiously and mumbled an apology, and then, calling to Russet, raced off along the
path. Edward turned his charming smile upon Perdita.

"Am I usurping *your* duties, ma'am, in calling him

to account? I am aware that only his lessons are my
concern, but since Miss Caterby's death he has been
largely in my care, and I seem to have acquired the
habit of correcting him in other matters also."

She murmured a hasty disclaimer, and since Melissa
had paused to gather some late roses, took the opportunity of asking whether the children had been or-
phaned very long ago. Edward nodded.

"Their father died shortly before Stephen was born,
and their mother survived the birth by only a few
weeks. Even Melissa can scarcely remember either
parent."

"Poor children!" Perdita said softly, and cast an involuntary glance at the great, sprawling mansion loom-
ing a short distance away. She had the impression that
Tarrington Chase was not a happy house, and her heart
went out to the boy and girl whose childhood was being
spent there, surrounded by wealth and luxury but denied real affection. She felt ashamed of her own antag-
onism towards Melissa, and resolved to do all she could
to win her friendship.

A possible reason for Melissa's hostility towards her
young governess was made apparent a few minutes
later. She came hastening after them with her hands
full of roses, but made no response when Perdita ad-
mired the flowers. Instead she held them up to her face,
looking up over them at Edward with an expression at
once shy and adoring, and Perdita realised with dismay
that Melissa was in the throes of a romantic infatuation. This was scarcely to be wondered at, since Mr
Eastly was a personable young man, but it was not
likely to make Perdita's task any easier.

They came back to the house by way of the spiral

stair, and as they reached the corridor above, Gwenny entered it from the other end.

"Nurse be asking to see you, miss," she informed Perdita. "Can you come to her now, if you please? Her ladyship do like folk to humour all the poor old soul's fancies."

"You had better go, Miss Frayne," Edward put in with a smile, seeing Perdita's bewilderment. "*I* was obliged to undergo the same scrutiny when I first arrived. Nurse has had charge of three generations of Tarringtons, for she was here when the children's grandfather, Sir Humphrey, was an infant, and though she is bedridden now, she still keeps a sharp eye on her one-time charges. I fear I did not altogether meet with her approval, but I am sure that you will fare better."

Perdita thought that so peremptory a summons from an old servant was rather curious, but as she was beginning to feel that nothing which happened at Tarrington Chase would surprise her, she followed Gwenny without argument. The girl led her to an entirely different part of the house, to a small but pleasant room overlooking the kitchen garden, with a glimpse of the dim blue plateau of the Forest away beyond the trees.

Propped against pillows in the high, narrow bed, covered by a brilliant patchwork quilt, was the oldest woman Perdita had ever seen. Her face, framed by an old-fashioned nightcap, was an incredible network of wrinkles, and the hands resting on the gay coverlet shrivelled to the semblance of a bird's claws, yet the faded eyes were bright and intelligent. They scanned Perdita from head to foot as she approached, and when she paused by the bed the shrewd, assessing gaze came to rest on her face, until she felt herself colouring beneath the intense regard.

"The new governess, eh?" Nurse remarked in a thin, quavering voice. "A slip of a lass scarce older than Miss Melissa! Times do be changed, indeed!"

"I am perhaps older than you think," Perdita replied with a smile, for she found it impossible to be vexed with this little, doll-like old woman, "and her ladyship feels it may be good for Miss Melissa to be in the care of someone near her own age."

"Aye, us be all old folk at the Chase!" Nurse agreed grimly. "All save the fine gentleman as do call hisself a tutor." She gave a derisive cackle of laughter. "Master Humphrey had tutors, long since, and so did Master Stephen, but none the likes o' that 'un!"

Perdita could find nothing to say in answer to this remark, which seemed to her to be wholly justified, so she remained silent. Nurse continued to study her with an oddly searching regard.

"You'm a pretty young thing!" she said abruptly after a pause. "Too pretty, mebbe, for your own good, but your eyes be honest. Honest and kind! So now mind what I do say." She leaned forward, one of her claw-like hands reaching out to clasp Perdita's wrist while the shrewd, faded eyes gazed intently into hers. "Evil do breed evil, and them as do hate cares naught who suffers, so long as their hate be satisfied."

"I do not understand you!" Perdita tried to speak coolly, wondering whether, in spite of her rational manner, the old woman were slightly mad. "Are you trying to warn me against something, or someone?"

"Evil do breed evil!" Nurse repeated. "There be a

shadow over this house, my dearie, and has been this
many a year, but now it do be growing darker. Him
have come back, him as us thought dead long since in
foreign parts."

"Him?" Perdita repeated, conscious of suddenly
quickened heartbeats. "Do you mean Mr Hawkesworth?"

"Aye, young Jason!" Nurse's fingers tightened about
her wrist. "My lady be afeared of him, for all her
anger, and so be I, for him be one as won't forgive nor
forget. You'm not to let him near the babbies, mind,
nor them near him!"

"But why?" Perdita insisted. "Surely you do not
think he would harm them."

"Never you mind why!" Nurse released her wrist
and sank back against the pillows, closing her eyes.
"Just do as you'm bid. There be good reason for it."

She refused to say any more, and Perdita returned to
the schoolroom more mystified than before. So Jason
Hawkesworth was not, as she had supposed, a stranger
who had lately settled in the village and was resented
on that account. The differences, whatever they were,
between him and Lady Tarrington were of long standing, and though Perdita felt inclined to dismiss Nurse's
fears as the fantasies of extreme age, she could not help
wondering what lay behind the mystery.

For the next few days she was fully occupied in
mastering the demands of her new post, and had little
leisure to think of anything else. Then, one afternoon,
she was summoned to Lady Tarrington's sitting-room,
where, after a few general remarks, her ladyship surprised her by asking:

"Are you capable of driving a carriage, Miss Frayne?"

"Yes, my lady. Towards the end of my father's life I was accustomed to drive him on his parish visits."

"Then tomorrow the gig will be brought round at two o'clock, and you will drive the children to the village. It is the anniversary of their father's death, and it is their custom to place flowers beneath the memorial to him which stands in the church. To the church only, Miss Frayne, and then straight home. You understand me?"

Perdita assured her that she did, and went back to the schoolroom. She found that she was looking forward to the proposed outing, brief though it was to be, for the oppressive grandeur of Tarrington Chase weighed heavily on her spirits. Only in the schoolroom wing did there seem to be any lightheartedness, and even that was marred by Melissa's secretive air and scarcely veiled hostility.

On the following day, when the gig was brought around, Perdita found that Stephen was watching her with some anxiety, for Russet was fastened beneath the seat. She felt a trifle dubious about allowing the dog to accompany them, but could not resist the appeal in the child's eyes.

"Get into the carriage, children," she said quietly. "Sir Stephen, there will not be a great deal of room, so you had better sit between your sister and me, and hold Russet on your lap."

He bestowed a beaming smile of gratitude upon her and scrambled up into the gig, Melissa and Perdita following. It was a breezy day of fitful sunshine, with the

3

cloud shadows sweeping across hill and valley so that
the aspect of the scene was constantly changing with
the changing light, but Perdita had little opportunity to
admire the view as they drove down the hill. The road
was not an easy one, and it was so long since she had
handled the reins that she was obliged to give all her
attention to her driving.

She breathed a sigh of relief when the bottom of the
hill was reached, and the road levelled out to join another which ran along the floor of the valley. When
they reached that point she heard a horse coming fast
along the other fork of the road, which was hidden
from her by a high bank, and she drew rein to let it
pass. The rider flashed into view, she caught a glimpse
of outlandish garments, and a dark, bearded face below
a brilliant turban, and then he passed out of sight again
round a bend in the road towards the village.

"That was Mr Hawkesworth's servant," Stephen explained, seeing Perdita's look of astonishment. "He
used to live in India, you know, and he made a great
fortune there, and he brought that man back with him.
His name is Mahdu, and they say he would do anything
in the world for Mr Hawkesworth, no matter how
wicked it might be. They say . . ."

"You have been listening to the servants' gossip
again, Stephen," Melissa broke in primly. "You know
that Grandmama has forbidden us to talk about that
man."

"I don't see why!" her brother retorted mutinously.
"I like talking about him! I would like to talk *to* him,
too, and ask him what it is like in India, and if he really did all the terrible things they say he did when he
was there. *I'm* not afraid of him!"

"If your grandmama has forbidden you to talk about Mr Hawkesworth, Sir Stephen, there is no more to be said," Perdita put in firmly. "Pray remember where we are going, and why, and endeavour to turn your thoughts in a more proper direction."

Crushed by this rebuke, Stephen subsided into rebellious silence, burying his face in Russet's silky fur and not speaking again until their destination was reached. The church stood on the same side of the river as Tarrington Chase, but beyond the village, on the crest of a knoll. A short, steep avenue of chestnut trees led to a grassy space before the lych-gate, and here they alighted and tethered the horse. Russet was tied again in his place beneath the seat, whining with dismay at being thus abandoned, and Perdita, taking up the flowers, followed her charges through the gate and along the path.

The churchyard here was a gloomy place, shadowed by huge and ancient yews, for this was the northern side of the church, unconsecrated ground where, according to the harsh old laws, lay buried unbaptised children and any unfortunate wretch desperate enough to commit suicide. Even on that summer afternoon a dismal air hung about it, the great trees shutting out the sunlight and stretching their dark branches above the graves.

The church itself was beautiful, small and old and rich with carved wood and stained glass. The name of Tarrington, and the coat of arms, were much in evidence, and for the first time Perdita realised how deeply the family had set its imprint upon this parish where for more than two centuries it had held undisputed sway. It was no wonder that, where Jason Hawkesworth was concerned, the villagers had taken their lead from the chatelaine of Tarrington Chase.

When the children had placed their flowers and said a prayer, they went out again into the churchyard. Melissa walked decorously at Perdita's side, but Stephen broke into a run along the path. Perdita called to him to stay, but he paid no heed and raced instead through the gateway towards the gig and his impatient pet.

Perdita's attention was distracted from her errant charge by a movement near one of the yew trees close by the churchyard wall. A man was standing there, where a new headstone showed in sharp contrast to the green-black foliage and the weathered, moss-grown wall. He was bare-headed, and had been looking down at the grave by which he stood, but at the sound of Perdita's voice he turned, and for the second time she found herself confronted by the dark, piratical face of Jason Hawkesworth.

III

When she looked towards him he did not, as most people would have done, glance away, but continued steadily to regard her. The hard, tawny eyes were utterly indifferent, but Perdita was somehow made suddenly aware of her shabby, unfashionable clothes and generally dowdy appearance, though these were matters which did not usually trouble her. She tilted her chin defiantly and quickened her pace, calling again, more severely, to Stephen.

The little boy was now standing on the step of the gig to untie Russet's leash, and gave no sign of having heard. As Perdita reached the gig, the dog leapt down and went scampering off, but when its young master would have followed she caught him by the arm. She

SYLVIA THORPE

was very angry, not so much because of Stephen's disobedience as because Hawkesworth was a witness of
her apparent inability to control the child.

"When I bid you do something, Sir Stephen," she
said sharply, giving his arm a little shake, "pray have
the goodness to obey me at once. I see that I was mistaken in allowing you to bring Russet with you, since
his presence prompts you to such unruly behaviour. I
shall certainly not permit it again."

He started to say something, but whether of protest
or excuse was never known, for he was interrupted by a
sudden commotion from the far side of the stretch of
grass, Russet's high-pitched, terrified yelping mingling
with deeper, more savage snarls. As the puppy reached
the trees another dog had leapt out upon it, a lean,
brindled cur with a narrow, evil head and viciously
flattened ears.

Stephen uttered a scream of horror and would have
rushed to rescue his pet, but Perdita's hold on his arm
prevented it. She said, with all the force she could
command:

"Stay there with your sister," and, thrusting him in
Melissa's direction, ran as fast as she could towards the
writhing, snarling dogs.

She was prevented in her turn. Jason Hawkesworth
had vaulted the low wall, and, reaching the spot at the
same moment, swung her unceremoniously aside. The
lash of his riding-whip cracked fiercely about the brindled dog's lean flanks, and with a yelp of pain and
fright it released its victim and bolted into the undergrowth from which it had emerged. Perdita, pale-faced
and shaken, said breathlessly:

"Oh, thank Heaven! I am very grateful to you, sir!"

"So you should be," he replied sardonically, "for you would undoubtedly have been badly bitten. Do you know no better, you little fool, than to try to stop a dog-fight with your bare hands?"

Words and tone slew every feeling of gratitude stone dead, and she looked up at him in speechless indignation. Standing thus near to him, she realised that he was even taller than he had seemed on horseback; although above average height herself she felt diminutive beside him, and the sensation did nothing to soothe her feelings. She said stiffly:

"I did not stop to consider that! Something had to be done, and I did not know that *you* would be obliging enough to intervene."

"Miss Frayne! Miss Frayne!" Stephen, on his knees beside his prostrate pet, tugged frantically at her skirts. "Russet is most dreadfully hurt!"

The little dog did indeed appear to be in a grievous state. It lay on its side, panting, its eyes half-shut, and on its neck the silky fur was wet with blood. As Perdita stared helplessly at it, knowing neither how to aid the animal nor to reassure its frightened, tearful owner, she heard Hawkesworth say something under his breath in a tone of the utmost exasperation. He spoke in a foreign tone, but from the way the words were uttered she thought they were very likely an oath. Then he addressed Stephen, more distinctly this time, and in English.

"Get up, boy, and stop blubbering! Only babes and weaklings weep! Here, hold these for me while I see what harm has been done."

He pulled off his gloves and thrust them, with his

whip, into Stephen's hands. Then, going down on one knee, he began to examine Russet's injuries with unexpectedly deft and gentle fingers. The puppy whimpered, but made no attempt to snap at him.

"It's a nasty bite," Jason said at length, "but I think he is more frightened than anything else. If you take my advice you will have Bryn Morgan look at him. He knows more about animals and the doctoring of them than any man in the county."

"Yes," Stephen said eagerly. "Yes, I will! Thank you, sir!"

It dawned suddenly upon Perdita, hitherto preoccupied with the sudden crisis, that she was permitting the very thing which Lady Tarrington had expressly forbidden, and allowing Jason Hawkesworth to talk to her charges—or, at least, to one of them. A glance over her shoulder showed that Melissa had climbed into the gig and was sitting there, her hands folded in her lap, gazing into the distance as though disassociating herself from the whole affair.

"We had better go," Perdita said uneasily. "Sir Stephen, you will have to carry Russet—or shall I do so for you?"

"No thank you. I will do it." Stephen handed Jason's property back to him and gathered his pet carefully into his arms. "Please hurry, ma'am!"

He went towards the gig, Perdita following, and to her surprise and dismay Jason went with them. He lifted boy and dog bodily into the carriage, and then turned to offer Perdita his hand to help her in also. She could not refuse without seeming churlish, although she was very conscious of Melissa's watchful sidelong glance, and could tell, from the mockery in Hawkesworth's eyes, that he was aware of it, too. She gathered up the reins.

"Thank you, sir," she said, as distantly as she could. "I am greatly obliged to you for your help."

"It was a pleasure, ma'am," he replied, with a courtesy as mocking as his look. He bowed slightly to Melissa. "Miss Tarrington!"

She flashed him one outraged glance and then turned her head away, not deigning to make any response, and Perdita saw a singularly saturnine smile touch Jason Hawkesworth's hard mouth. He stepped back, and the gig moved off.

The first part of the return journey was accomplished in a silence broken only by Russet's occasional whimpers, but as they began the long ascent of Tarrington Chase Melissa said primly, but on an undeniable note of triumph:

"Grandmama will be most displeased, Stephen, when she hears that you have been talking to that man."

Her brother looked up. "Why should she hear? *I* shall not tell her."

"Then it will be my duty to do so!" Melissa announced. "One should always endeavour to do one's duty, should one not, Miss Frayne?"

Appealed to in this sly fashion, Perdita did not know how to reply. She had been in no way to blame for the meeting with Hawkesworth, but that fact was unlikely to weigh with Lady Tarrington.

"One should certainly so endeavour, Miss Tarrington," she agreed at length, "but I believe that one should first be quite certain where one's duty lies."

"On this occasion," Melissa said airily, "there can surely be no doubt of that."

"You're a mean cat, Melissa," Stephen told her angrily. "You know Grandmama will blame Miss Frayne, and it wasn't her fault. If Mr Hawkesworth hadn't been there, Russet would have been killed."

"I am surprised," Melissa said righteously, "that you allow that to influence you. Have you forgotten that that man was the cause of the injuries you suffered last spring?"

"That was an accident," Stephen replied indifferently. "Please, Miss Frayne, can we not go faster?"

Since the horse was already making its best possible speed up the long, steep hill, Perdita was obliged to point out that they could not, and he subsided into anxious silence, cradling the injured puppy tenderly in his arms with no regard for the dirt and blood which stained his clothes. Perdita wondered what lay behind the reference to an accident, but thought it best to ask no questions.

They had passed the hairpin bend and were halfway along the upper stretch of road when they saw Edward Eastly, mounted on a fine bay mare, coming towards them at a brisk trot. As he drew near he lifted his hat in smiling greeting, then, seeing the state Stephen was in, abruptly drew rein.

"What has been happening?" he asked sharply.

Between them, they told him. Edward looked searchingly at Perdita, perceived the anxiety she was trying to disguise, and said briefly to Melissa:

"Why are you so determined to carry tales to your grandmother?"

A flush of mortification rose to Melissa's pale cheeks, for, put like that, the matter sounded very different from the way she had expressed it. She started to stammer her previous excuse about duty, but he cut in without ceremony.

"That sounds very fine, but consider for a moment whether it is, in fact, your duty to tell your grandmother something which cannot fail to distress her. The incident, for which no one was to blame, is over, and it would be more charitable to allow it to be forgotten." He paused, and then added, in a tone which from minatory had become persuasive: "Only a very mean-spirited person would do otherwise, and you are not mean-spirited, are you, Melissa?"

Perdita thought it extremely unlikely that Melissa would succumb to this mixture of sternness and smiling cajolery, but apparently Edward had gauged the girl's nature more accurately than she had done, for after only the smallest hesitation, Melissa said slowly:

"If *you* feel that nothing should be said to Grandmama, Edward, then no doubt it should not. I am sure I have no wish to distress her."

"Oh, please, must we stay here talking?" Stephen broke in in an anguished tone. "Russet is still bleeding, and I am so afraid he will die!"

"No, of course not," Edward agreed at once. "I will ride back to the house, Stephen, and send someone to find Bryn Morgan. It is true that he is the best person to look after your dog."

He wheeled his mount and rode off at a canter, soon to be lost to view over the brow of the hill. Perdita, urging their own horse in the same direction, asked curiously:

"Who *is* Bryn Morgan?"

Melissa made a little grimace. "He is a horrid, dirty old man who lives all alone in a cottage in the Lower

Wood, and poaches game from the preserves, and salmon from the river. If the cottage belonged to us, Grandmama would turn him out."

"I like Bryn," Stephen said defiantly. "He knows everything about animals. He even keeps a tame fox as a pet."

"He is like an animal himself," Melissa retorted with a fastidious shudder. "I do not know how you can bear to have anything to do with him—especially as the only person for whom he has any real regard is that man."

Perdita assumed that this was another reference to Jason Hawkesworth, since Melissa seemed determined not to utter his name. It seemed to be of a piece with all the rest, she reflected, that the only person in the neighbourhood with whom Hawkesworth appeared to be on friendly terms was a disreputable old poacher.

When they reached the house, Stephen was with difficulty persuaded to hand Russet over to the care of one of the grooms, to look after until Bryn Morgan arrived. Perdita thought it best to keep the little boy away from the kennel for the rest of the afternoon, and she and Melissa did their best to keep him occupied, but he was restless and on edge, unable to take much interest in anything. Perdita wondered anxiously what the effect on him would be if his pet died, and was almost as relieved as he was when, at about five o'clock, Edward came into the schoolroom and said cheerfully:

"You may set your mind at ease about Russet, Stephen! Morgan has seen him, and says that there is no great harm done. In a few days the little fellow will be as lively as ever."

An expression of rapturous joy flooded into Stephen's face, and he jumped up, begging permission to go to the kennel at once. Perdita gave it smilingly; he raced from the room, and they heard him go clattering at reckless speed along the corridor and down the spiral stair. Edward glanced at Melissa.

"He gave me no time to say that the dog must not be excited," he remarked. "You had better go after him, Melissa, and warn him."

With obvious reluctance she got up and went slowly from the room, casting a resentful glance back from the threshold and pointedly leaving the door wide open. Edward went across and shut it.

"Melissa has a very strong sense of propriety," he said with some amusement, "due largely to the influence of your predecessor. It is plain she does not think that governess and tutor should be allowed to discuss their pupils in private."

To her vexation, Perdita felt the colour rising to her cheeks. She was not at all certain that Melissa's feelings on that score were wrong, and wished that Mr Eastly conformed more closely to the conventional idea of a tutor. With his well-cut clothes and air of quiet assurance, he seemed more like a son of the house.

"I was not aware, sir," she said in her primmest tone, "that we have anything *to* discuss."

"Not about the children," he agreed quietly, "but I feel that some explanation of my own position in this house is due to you, and since no one else is likely to offer it, you must forgive me if I talk about myself for a few moments."

Perdita started to protest, embarrassed by the thought that her curiosity had been so apparent, but he would not let her go on.

"I am well aware, Miss Frayne, that since you and I

occupy similar positions in this house, it must seem strange to you that Lady Tarrington treats me with a consideration not offered to you. The fact is that her ladyship and my father are very old friends. They grew up together, and it is to that long-standing friendship that I owe my present post as tutor to Stephen. Being the youngest of a considerable family, I am obliged to earn my own living, but it pleases Lady Tarrington to treat me as a guest rather than as a mere dependent."

"Mr Eastly, I assure you there is no need to tell me this," Perdita said uncomfortably. "It is not for me to question her ladyship's bearing towards either of us."

"I think there was every need," he said with a smile, "but now my conscience is clear on that score, and since I can see that the subject is distasteful to you, I will say no more. You have had a sufficiently trying afternoon without my adding to it."

"It was very disturbing," she agreed, "but I am thankful that Russet suffered no serious injury. Sir Stephen is so greatly attached to his pet that I fear the effect might have proved disastrous had the little dog died."

"He is a great deal *too* deeply attached to it, ma'am," Edward replied bluntly. "The truth is that Stephen lacks the companionship a boy should have. This is no life for him, isolated here with his grandmother and sister. He will be far better off when he goes to Eton."

"Is he going there, sir?" Perdita asked in surprise. "I did not realise that."

"In a year's time," Edward explained. "That is why I am here to coach him. Miss Caterby was an excellent woman, and expert at teaching young ladies fashionable accomplishments, but she had not the qualifications to prepare a boy for his public school." He paused, and then added humorously: "Neither did she possess the youth and good looks to make Jason Hawkesworth leap to her assistance, but in this household that was an advantage. Do you know, Miss Frayne, what would have happened if Melissa had been allowed to carry *that* tale to her grandmother?"

Perdita looked indignantly at him. "I do know, sir, and I am aware I must be grateful to you for persuading Miss Tarrington to remain silent, but I do not think I care for the tone of your remark. Mr Hawkesworth's presence, providential though it was, was wholly fortuitous!"

Edward laughed. "My dear ma'am, I was not implying that you had an assignation with him! If Lady Tarrington has spoken to you concerning the fellow, you have no need of warnings from me, but pray believe that I offered one only to save you from offending through ignorance."

He spoke with such sincerity that Perdita immediately regretted the way in which she had snubbed him, and said more warmly:

"You are very kind, sir, and I truly am grateful. It means a great deal to me to retain her ladyship's good opinion."

"I have every confidence, ma'am, that you will retain it," he replied with a smile, "as long as you avoid Jason Hawkesworth. Make no mistake, he is a dangerous man!"

She looked at him in astonishment, thinking he must be jesting, but saw at once that he spoke in all seriousness. He would say no more, however, and almost im-

mediately made some excuse to leave her, as though he
regretted having said so much. Perdita, left alone to
ponder his words, did so with some perplexity. She
could think of a number of words which might have
been used to describe Mr Hawkesworth—rude, over-
bearing, infuriating, were only a few of them—but to
call him dangerous seemed to her to be something of
an exaggeration.

The next day was Sunday, and Perdita accompanied
her charges and their grandmother to church. That is to
say, the children went in Lady Tarrington's carriage
with her ladyship and Mr Eastly, and Perdita followed
in the big, old-fashioned coach with the housekeeper,
Mrs Price, and other upper servants. In the church, a
similar pattern was followed. The old lady went in on
Edward's arm, her grandchildren following, and entered the Tarrington pew, which was an enormous affair with high wooden sides to screen its occupants
from the rest of the congregation; Perdita sat with Mrs
Price, farther back.

There was another pew, similar in style to that occupied by Lady Tarrington, on the other side of the aisle.
It was empty when the party from Tarrington Chase
arrived, but after a few minutes Perdita became aware
of a stir passing through the assembled villagers, a
slight but perceptible ripple of sound and movement
oddly suggestive of resentment. Footsteps rang on the
stone paving, and she looked up to see Jason Hawkesworth go past and enter the second pew.

He was not alone. Leaning on his arm was a lady;
young, blonde, very good-looking and exquisitely
dressed. Even Perdita, who made all her own gowns
and had only on rare occasions seen fashion-plates in

ladies' periodicals, could tell that those deceptively simple garments had probably cost a small fortune. She regarded them with an admiration not entirely free from envy, and reflected rather waspishly that Mrs Hawkesworth—for that, presumably, was who the lady was—had shown better taste in choosing her clothes than in choosing a husband.

When the service was over, the congregation waited respectfully for Lady Tarrington to leave the church first, but as she stepped from her pew, Jason Hawkesworth emerged from his. For a second or two they confronted each other, and then with a bow and a wave of his hand he invited her ladyship to precede him. It was, on the face of it, a mere formal courtesy, but Perdita saw that the old lady's thin, colourless face was as rigid as stone, while into Hawkesworth's dark countenance had come the same look of saturnine mockery she had seen there when Melissa deliberately ignored him.

Curiosity, and impatience to solve the mystery, bubbled up within her, though she knew that in her position she would be prudent to subdue such feelings. As she walked with Mrs Price along the path to the lychgate, she looked surreptitiously towards the grave where she had seen Jason standing with such obvious reverence the day before. It was some yards away, but Perdita's eyesight was good, and the lettering on the headstone newly cut, so that she could read the brief, bald inscription with very little difficulty. It consisted simply of a name and two dates—"Susan Hawkesworth, 1758-1806".

Perdita went on through the gate and climbed into the coach with even more questions than before seeth-

ing in her mind. Who was Susan Hawkesworth? His
sister, perhaps? Then a swift calculation based on the
two dates told her that this was unlikely, since Jason
himself could not be more than thirty-five at the most.
Yet whoever Susan Hawkesworth was, why had she
been buried in that desolate corner of the churchyard,
and her grave left unmarked for six years—for the
headstone was obviously new? And Jason had the
tawny Tarrington eyes, and a courtesy from him
enraged Lady Tarrington as much as an insult from
anyone else. . . .

Perdita's curiosity was now too great to be denied,
but she still had caution enough to approach the subject obliquely. Watching Jason's fashionable open carriage going away down the steep lane beneath the
chestnut trees, she remarked to the housekeeper:

"Mrs Hawkesworth is extremely handsome, is she
not?"

The woman looked blankly at her for a second or
two, and then an expression of grim disapproval came
into her face. "If you mean, miss, the young woman
who came into church on Jason Hawkesworth's arm,
that's Miss Delamere. There's no Mrs Hawkesworth."

"Oh!" Perdita felt rather foolish. "I assumed that
she was his wife."

Mrs Price pursed her lips primly. "She's that in all
but name! The impudence of the man, bringing her
into church among decent, respectable folk! I never
knew the like!"

"That be the only way he *will* take her to church,
you mark my words!" the head footman put in with a
grin. "When he came to Mays Court last year he had a
dark, foreign piece in keeping, and they do say . . . !"

He caught Mrs Price's eye, and subsided into silence under its frosty stare.

"That's no way to talk in front of Miss Frayne," she said reprovingly. "Not but what it's as well for you to know the facts, miss, though it don't do to speak of 'em up at the Chase. The goings-on at Mays Court are no concern of anyone there, I'm glad to say!"

This would have been an excellent opening for further inquiries, but Perdita, still sunk in scarlet-cheeked confusion at the result of her first remark, was too embarrassed to take advantage of it. She was not unaware of the existence of such irregular relationships, but she had been brought up in the belief that they must always be ignored by any woman with pretensions to gentility. At that moment, nothing in the world could have persuaded her to ask anything else.

So the mystery surrounding Jason Hawkesworth remained a mystery to her, though it soon became obvious that the master of Mays Court provided a fertile topic of conversation for the servants at Tarrington Chase, and that Gwenny was the most avid gossip of them all. Her family lived in the village and she visited them once a week, and it did not take Perdita long to find out where Stephen obtained his information about Mr Hawkesworth.

She felt it to be her duty to rebuke Gwenny for encouraging the little boy's curiosity, since this was expressly forbidden by his grandmother, but she had little hope of being attended to. Stephen was apparently fascinated by the subject, and especially by the Indian servant, Mahdu. Perdita considered this natural enough, but, being certain that Lady Tarrington would not agree, lived in constant dread that she would dis-

cover it. Her own position at Tarrington Chase was so
precarious that the fear of losing it, and finding herself
alone and friendless in this wild part of the country,
was always with her.

IV

The first of September was Stephen's birthday, and to mark the occasion he and his sister were to be released from their usual routine of lessons. Instead, Lady Tarrington was taking them to visit some friends who lived a few miles away, and as Edward was to accompany them, Perdita was looking forward to a day entirely to herself.

She felt in need of it. During the short time she had been at Tarrington Chase she had grown very fond of Stephen, for he was an engaging child, lively and intelligent, with an open, affectionate nature which was in direct contrast to his sister's sly, secretive ways and overwhelming sense of her own importance. Perdita marvelled sometimes that brother and sister could be so unlike, for, still trying in vain to establish a friendly relationship with the girl, and to bear patiently ceaseless, unfavourable comparisons between her own ways and those of her predecessor, she had been brought to the brink of despair. She felt sometimes that if Melissa said once more: "But Miss Caterby always . . ." she would not be able to control her temper. Yet control it she must, for she felt quite certain that Melissa was only waiting for some valid cause for complaint to carry tales to her grandmother.

September the first was a day of intermittent sunshine, with a westerly gale blustering across the hills. Stephen, who had been in dread of wet weather which would prevent the promised outing, was up an hour before his usual time and out in the gardens with Russet, and by the time he came in to breakfast, windswept and rather grubby, Gwenny had carried into the schoolroom all the presents which had been sent to him. These were numerous, for besides those from his grandmother and sister, and one sent from Cheltenham Spa by his maternal grandparents, there were others from servants and tenants. Perdita, going into the schoolroom, found him delving gleefully into a box of sugar-plums, and was obliged to reprove him.

"I have only eaten two, Miss Frayne," he assured her earnestly. "Would you like one?"

"Not before breakfast, I thank you," she replied, suppressing a smile, "and you will have no more at present, either. Do you wish to make yourself unwell, and be unable to go with your grandmama and sister?"

"I told him not to eat them," Melissa said virtuously, "but they are his favourite sweetmeat, and he would take no notice."

"Then it is fortunate that I came in when I did," Perdita said firmly, taking the box from him. "You may have some more, Sir Stephen, when you come home this evening."

She put the box away in a cupboard, and Stephen, accepting this with equanimity, begged her to come and look at his other gifts. She was still admiring these when Gwenny came in with the breakfast, and something to tell which instantly diverted his thoughts.

"What do you think, miss!" she exclaimed, obviously bursting to share her news. "That blackamoor o' Mr Hawkesworth's were in the gardens this very morning! Did you ever know such impudence?"

"In the gardens?" Perdita repeated disbelievingly. "Gwenny, are you sure?"

"Sure as I do stand here, miss! Two o' the gardeners saw 'un at the far end o' the Long Walk, and Mr Eastly caught a glimpse of 'un going into the wood. There be no mistaking them queer clothes him do wear, and that coloured thing on his head."

"*I* did not see him," Stephen said disconsolately. "Oh, how I wish I had! I have never seen him really close, and today I could even have spoken to him, had I known he was here!"

"Lord, sir, you don't want naught to do wi' a nasty blackamoor!" Gwenny exclaimed in a shocked tone. "Him do fair make my flesh creep every time I do see 'un, and as for talking to 'un—well now, how could you, when you don't know the heathenish tongue him do speak?" To Perdita she added in a lower tone: "Her ladyship do be that angry about it, you'd never believe!"

Perdita had no difficulty in believing it, but what she

did find hard to credit was the truth of the story. Later, however, when Edward came to the schoolroom, he confirmed what Gwenny had said.

"Yes, I saw him quite distinctly. I was taking a stroll before breakfast, and the fellow was going along the path to the Lower Wood. I called to him to stop, intending to question what he was doing there, but he paid no heed, and though I followed I could find no trace of him."

"But what in the world would bring him here?" Perdita asked in a puzzled tone.

Edward shrugged. "Hawkesworth and Bryn Morgan are old cronies, so the Indian might have been going to Morgan's cottage, and mistaken the path. I can think of no other explanation."

Neither, it seemed, could anyone else, and the mystery of Mahdu's unexpected appearance had to remain unsolved. Gwenny and one or two of the other women servants professed alarm at the thought of "the blackamoor" being in the vicinity, but Perdita could see no reason to suppose that there was anything sinister about it. Most probably Edward was right, and the man had simply lost his way.

She certainly did not intend to remain cooped up indoors on his account, and that afternoon set out for a walk. She was in a mood of black depression, for Melissa had been more than usually difficult right up until the time she left the house, and Perdita was beginning to think that there was no smallest hope of ever winning her over.

The gale had abated none of its violence, but the gardens and the park were sheltered, and even, when the sun shone, pleasantly warm. For some time Perdita

walked about them, but then her restlessness tempted
her to venture into the woods beyond, along a grassy
ride which deteriorated after a while into a narrow,
gradually climbing path twisting this way and that
among the trees. Deep in troubled thought, she followed it with little regard for where it was leading her;
in the ordinary way she might have been nervous of the
wildness and loneliness of her surroundings, but at
present her one desire was to get as far away from the
house as possible, and solitude exactly suited her
mood.

It was very still in the woods, though the gale surged
in the branches overhead with a sound like distant surf,
and it was that ceaseless, restless roaring, as much as
her preoccupation, which prevented her from becoming
aware of voices close at hand until she rounded a bend
in the path and came face to face with the speakers.

They were Jason Hawkesworth and a little, wiry,
roughly-clad old man as gnarled and brown as the
trees around him, with bright, dark eyes in a face wrin-
kled like a walnut. So sudden and unexpected was the
encounter that Perdita gasped and stopped short, and
for a few seconds she and the two men stared at each
other in equal astonishment. Jason was the first to recover; he swept off his hat, and bowed.

"My dear Miss Frayne, this is an unlooked-for pleasure!" His tone was sardonic; the tawny eyes bright
with mockery. "And without your tiresome charges,
too! Strange! I had an idea they never left your side."

Perdita inclined her head coldly in response to the
greeting, but looked indignantly at him none the less.
She would have liked to walk straight on with no more
acknowledgment of his presence than that, but he was

standing in the middle of the path and showing no immediate intention of stepping aside. To thrust past him would be undignified; to turn back would savour of flight. Perdita stayed where she was, assuming an expression of impatient disdain.

This was wasted on Mr Hawkesworth. Looking ironically down at her, he said abruptly: "Bryn tells me the puppy recovered."

"Yes, sir, I thank you!" Perdita spoke curtly, though she could not forbear glancing quickly at the old man, apparently the notorious Bryn Morgan. "Mr Hawkesworth, will you be good enough to allow me to pass?"

"No, ma'am, I will not! I am of the opinion that you should go no farther."

Perdita gasped. "You take a great deal upon yourself, sir! By what right do you decide where I shall or shall not walk? This is, I believe, Tarrington land."

"It is common land, Miss Frayne," he retorted. "You crossed the boundary of the Tarrington Home Park some way back. I am sorry to disappoint you! You must have been looking forward to telling your employer that I had been trespassing, and now you find that I have a perfect right to be here."

"Would it make any difference if you had not?" she countered swiftly, and saw real amusement drive the mockery from his eyes.

"Not in the least," he replied cheerfully, "and I still do not intend to allow you to go on alone. You might come to harm."

"Pray do not be absurd!" she said angrily. "I have been walking quite safely through these woods until this moment, and there is not the least reason why I should not continue to do so. Now let me pass! If this is common land, you have no right to stop me!"

He laughed. "So the meek little governess has a temper! I would never have guessed it!" He stepped aside, and indicated the path with a wave of the hand which still held his hat. "As you say, ma'am, I have no right to stop you! The way is open!"

Perdita walked past him with her head very erect. She heard Bryn Morgan say something she could not catch, and Hawkesworth laughed again. Her cheeks burned, for she felt certain that the laughter was at her expense.

As she walked briskly on, wondering now where the path would lead her, and—uneasily—whether she would have to return the same way and again run the gauntlet of Mr Hawkesworth's mockery if he still chanced to be there, she heard a twig snap sharply beneath a foot just behind her. Swinging round, she saw Jason himself a yard or two away. She uttered a gasp of indignation, but the protest she was about to make was forestalled.

"Common land, Miss Frayne!" he reminded her ironically. "If I choose to walk along this path, you have no right to stop me."

To have her own words tossed back at her in that fashion was the most infuriating thing she could imagine, and it left her at a loss for words. She could only cast him a glance eloquent of all the things she was too ladylike to utter, which made him laugh again, and walk on, doing her best to ignore his presence.

She was too angry now to care where the path led, but this she was soon to discover. The woods ended abruptly, with no hedge or wall to mark their boundary. One moment the path was a tunnel amid trees and undergrowth, the next it had lost itself in bare rock. She was out in the open before she realised it, and the wind struck her with the force of a solid thing, driving the breath from her body and sending her staggering before it. She was almost swept off her feet, and knew a moment's blind panic before she felt herself steadied by a reassuringly strong arm.

"Take care!" Jason's deep, sardonic voice spoke close to her ear. "This is no place to tread unwarily."

Gasping and blinking, she looked about her and saw that he spoke the truth. They had emerged on to an outcrop of rock which jutted from the hill like the prow of a ship. Before them, the ground sloped very slightly upward for a score of feet and then ceased abruptly, and at its broadest point could be no more than three or four yards wide. Beyond that little platform of rock was emptiness, save for the countryside spread out, mile on rolling mile, beyond and below. On one hand, the tree-clad heights of the forest, its wild solitudes guarded by towering cliffs, and the turbulent river which writhed crazily along the foot of them. On the other side of the river, the fertile valley, soon bounded by other hills, range on blue range as far as the eye could see. Cloud shadows raced across it, as the clouds themselves raced across the sky, and always there was the fierce wind, blinding, buffeting, driving the breath back into her throat . . .

"We call this place the Spur," Jason said above the sound of it. "Its walls fall almost sheer for three hundred feet on every side save that by which we approached. Do you understand now why I did not mean to let you come here alone on such a day?"

Perdita nodded. She had no breath with which to reply. The wind flattened her clothes coldly against her body, tore off her bonnet so that it hung by its strings behind her shoulders, whipped her hair loose about her face. Alone on that dizzy height in such a gale she would have been terrified, but as it was she felt only a strange exultation. The unleashed force of the wind seemed to sweep away her doubts and depression, and woke a response from some unsuspected wildness deep within her. She laughed aloud with delight, almost without being aware of it, and lifted her head to look up at her companion.

His arm was still around her—she had accepted its support without question—and just for an instant she looked into the dark face and gold-brown eyes close above her own. Then his hold on her tightened, he bent his head and kissed her, long and hard, on the lips.

For a second or two, shock held her motionless before she started to struggle. He let her go, and she broke away to stumble back into the shelter of the trees. As suddenly as it had struck her, the wild wind was left behind, and she leaned against a tree-trunk and hid her face in the crook of her arm, shaking with anger and humiliation.

A movement close by made her aware that he had followed her, and she looked up in swift alarm. He rested his hand against the tree and grinned at her. His black hair was tousled by the wind, and in spite of his fashionable clothes he looked like a gipsy, disreputable and dangerous.

"No need to be so frightened," he said ironically. "Your virtue is in no immediate danger, I assure you!"

"Oh, you are unspeakable!" she said in a trembling voice. "You think that because I am a mere governess you may treat me as you please, insult me by word and act . . ."

"Rid yourself of the notion that being a governess has anything to do with it," he interrupted with some amusement. "I could never feel the slightest desire to make love to the prim and proper Miss Frayne! But it was not Miss Frayne who stood laughing yonder. It was . . ." He broke off. "What *is* your given name?"

Perdita gasped. "That, sir, is no concern of yours!"

He shrugged. "As you please! I shall discover it for myself if I choose. Well, Miss Frayne, what now? Do you intend to complain to your employer about my shocking conduct? She will be only too ready to take the insult personally."

He still spoke lightly, but now there was an underlying savageness in his voice which she remembered later and puzzled over. At that moment, she was still too shaken to feel perplexity.

"Certainly not!" she said in an attempt at dignity. "I would not dream of mentioning so shameful an incident to anyone, least of all to Lady Tarrington. I shall endeavour to forget the disagreeable experience."

This damping remark had no visible effect on Mr Hawkesworth's self-assurance. He continued to watch her, his eyes filled with laughter, as she pulled on her bonnet and bundled her hair up anyhow under it. She tried to appear unconscious of his regard, but her

trembling fingers made a wretched business of tying the
strings, and the maddening, mocking voice said lightly:

"May I offer my assistance?"

She flashed him a glance of mingled anger and
alarm, and started to walk back along the path as
quickly as the uneven ground permitted. She was aware
of him following her, but he said no more, and when
they reached the spot where they had met, the sound of
his footsteps ceased. Perdita walked on without a pause
until she reached the bend, but then succumbed to the
temptation to look back. Standing where she had first
seen him—there was now no sign of Bryn Morgan—he
raised his hand in a careless gesture of farewell. She
made no response, but hurried on with her cheeks
burning again.

When she reached the house she went in by way of
the spiral stair, thankful that this enabled her to reach
her room without meeting anyone. Taking off her bonnet, she combed out her tangled hair and dressed it
again in its usual uncompromising style, but as she slid
the last pin into place, Jason's words flashed through
her mind. "The prim and proper Miss Frayne." That
was how she looked, with her severely dressed hair and
drab, unfashionable gown; how she ought to look,
surely, as governess to a well-bred young lady?

Yet though she now looked again as she always
sought to do, she still felt like a stranger to herself, and
she knew that she would not forget what had happened
that afternoon; that she would not even try to forget.
She had once had a similar experience forced upon her
by Henry Mulstead, and even now could not recall it
without a shiver of distaste, but she had felt no such

revulsion from Jason Hawkesworth. It was perhaps fortunate, she reflected soberly, that circumstances made any future meeting with him extremely unlikely.

By the time the children returned she had recovered at least an outward composure, but none the less was thankful to find that they were both so tired that she could pack them off to bed as soon as supper was over. When they had gone, she settled herself in the schoolroom to prepare Melissa's lessons for the following day, but her mind refused to remain on her work. The memory of a dark face and deep, amused voice kept intruding upon her thoughts, until in exasperation she put her books away and went to bed.

In a confused dream of high, windswept woods she heard someone calling her name, and woke with the sound of it ringing in her ears. After a few bewildered moments she realised that the cry was real, save that in her dream the voice had been Hawkesworth's, and in reality it was Stephen's, plaintive and sobbing, rising suddenly to an anguished scream. In alarm she sprang out of bed, fumbled her feet into slippers and caught up a shawl to cast about her shoulders as she ran from the room. Snatching up the small lamp which was left burning all night on a shelf in the corridor, she hurried into the child's room.

He was writhing among the tumbled bedclothes, clutching his stomach and moaning with pain. He seemed incapable of answering her anxious questions, and as she bent over him, Melissa came running into the room, saying in a frightened voice:

"What is it? What is the matter?"

"Your brother is ill," Perdita said shortly. "Stephen

dear, try to tell me! How long have you had a pain? Have you been sick?"

He shook his head, but Melissa, who had come to the other side of the bed, said in an altered voice: "I would not be surprised if he had, greedy little beast! Look, Miss Frayne! He has eaten all those sugar-plums!"

She pulled the empty box from behind the pillow and held it up, but at the same moment Stephen stiffened and screamed in another spasm of pain, and Perdita knew with sudden, fearful certainty that this was more than the just consequences of greediness. She said urgently:

"Is there a doctor within reach?"

"Yes, Dr Meredith lives in the village, but Grandmama might not wish you to . . ."

"I will ring for Gwenny," Perdita interrupted. "Stay with your brother until she comes and then go and wake Lady Tarrington."

Without waiting for a reply she ran from the room, and after tugging urgently at the bell-rope in the schoolroom, flew along the corridor and down the spiral stair. A brief struggle with the bolts, and then she was out in the open, running as fast as she could through the fitful moonlight to the cottage of the head groom, adjoining the stableyard.

Reaching it, she hammered frantically on the door until a casement opened above her and a head was thrust out, inquiring, with annoyance and alarm, what was wrong. Perdita stepped back a little and looked up.

"Sir Stephen is desperately ill! Fetch the doctor as fast as you can."

5

With a startled exclamation the head was withdrawn, and Perdita returned to the house. When, shivering with cold, she reached Stephen's room again, she found the frightened Gwenny trying in vain to soothe him. As Perdita joined her by the bed, she straightened up and said in a whisper:

"Him do be getting worse all the time, miss! What ails 'un?"

Perdita shook her head. "I wish to Heaven I knew, Gwenny! He seemed quite well when he went to bed."

Lady Tarrington, with a dressing-robe over her nightgown and a close-fitting cap hiding her hair, came hurrying in with Melissa at her heels. After one horrified glance at the writhing, sobbing child, she said sharply:

"Dr Meredith must be sent for!"

"I have already done so, my lady," Perdita replied. "I thought the matter too urgent to await your consent."

"Quite right, Miss Frayne!" She bent over Stephen, who for the moment lay still, whimpering quietly, his hair clinging damply to his forehead, his golden-brown eyes dull with pain. "There, my dearest, Grandmama is here now, and Dr Meredith is on his way. You will soon be better."

He clutched at her hand and clung to it as she seated herself in the chair which Gwenny had hastened to set beside the bed. "I should not have eaten all those sugar-plums," he moaned. "Miss Frayne told me not to. I'm sorry, Grandmama!"

She made some soothing reply, and he closed his eyes, lying quietly for so long that Perdita began to wonder whether she had given way to unnecessary

panic and roused the whole household without real
cause. Then, without warning, the pain took him again
and he began to scream. Melissa, who had apparently
been sharing Perdita's doubts, started to cry noisily,
and Lady Tarrington, gathering her grandson into her
arms, glanced up to say quietly:

"Take Melissa to her room, Miss Frayne, and stay
with her until she is calm. I will look after Stephen."

Perdita put her arm round the girl and led her from
the room, reflecting that whatever Lady Tarrington's
faults, she did not lose her head in an emergency. Melissa allowed herself to be helped back to bed, but proceeded to indulge in a fit of hysteria, though Perdita
could not help wondering how much of this was due to
concern for her brother, and how much to draw attention to herself. It took a long time to pacify her, but at
length she exhausted herself so completely that she fell
asleep, and Perdita was able to creep wearily from the
room.

A light was burning in the schoolroom, and through
the open door she could see Gwenny stooping to tend
the fire which had been kindled in the grate. The sight
of the leaping flames made Perdita realise how cold she
was, and she went thankfully into the room, saying in a
low voice:

"Gwenny, how is Sir Stephen? Is the doctor here?"

She broke off with a gasp, for Edward was standing
by the table in the middle of the room. His face looked
white and strained, and though he was fully dressed, his
clothes had obviously been flung on with none of the
usual fastidiousness, for his fair hair was rumpled and
his neckcloth tied in a careless knot. He came towards
her, saying in answer to her question:

"He has been here some time, but he is still with Stephen and there is no news yet. Lady Tarrington is with them." He looked searchingly at Perdita's white face. "My dear ma'am, you are quite worn out! Come to the fire."

She shook her head and clutched her shawl about her, acutely aware of her unconventional attire. "I must dress," she murmured confusedly. "There has been no time. I did not know that you were here."

She fled to her room, and with trembling hands hurried into her clothes and pinned up her hair. On her way back to the schoolroom she hesitated for a little outside Stephen's door, from beyond which came an indistinguishable murmur of voices, but fear of what she might find within, as much as fear of incurring Lady Tarrington's displeasure, held her back from entering.

Edward was alone in the schoolroom, sitting by the fire, and he rose at once to place a chair for her. A tray bearing decanter and glasses stood on the table, and he poured some of the wine and brought it to her.

"I had Gwenny fetch this," he said. "You need something to restore you."

She eyed the glass doubtfully. "You are very kind, sir, but I hardly think—"

"Take it, Miss Frayne," he interrupted quietly. "You have had a severe shock, and it will help nobody if you collapse."

She felt too worn out to argue, so she took the glass and sipped reluctantly at its contents, while Edward returned to his chair. Slowly the time crept by. Now and then they heard the hushed voices of servants in the corridor, and their hurrying footsteps, and each time grew tense and anxious, waiting fearfully for news which did not come. Once or twice Edward got up to pace restlessly about the room. They scarcely spoke, but Perdita was thankful for his presence; she felt that she could not have kept this long, anxious vigil alone.

At last, when the sky was lightening towards the dawn, they heard the door of Stephen's room open and close, and then footsteps, and Lady Tarrington came wearily into the room. She was followed by a small, middle-aged man with a thin, kindly face, and dark hair grizzled at the temples. The old lady looked utterly exhausted, but in answer to Edward's anxious question —Perdita could not bring herself to speak—she said in a voice hoarse with fatigue:

"He will live! By the mercy of God, he will live!"

"By the mercy of God, and this young lady's quick wits," Dr Meredith added, looking at Perdita. "It was you, ma'am, was it not, who sent so promptly to summon me?" She nodded wordlessly, and he added in a serious voice: "The boy owes his life to you. I was only just in time."

Edward had gone to Lady Tarrington, helping her solicitously to one of the chairs by the fire, and fetching her some wine. She patted his hand gratefully as she took the glass, but looked towards the doctor.

"You said, Dr Meredith, that there is something you wish to tell us."

"Yes, my lady, there is," he replied. "I wish I could spare you, but I dare not. It must be said."

Perdita looked at him in alarm, for the gravity in his voice, and in his kind, tired face, struck her with a sudden chill of foreboding. Edward said quickly:

"Sir, Lady Tarrington has endured a great deal to-night. Can this matter not wait until she has rested?"

"No, Mr Eastly, it cannot!" The doctor's voice was grim. "What I must tell her brooks no delay." He paused for a moment, looking from one to the other, and then added heavily: "That unfortunate child has been deliberately poisoned!"

V

Perdita felt the floor heave beneath her feet, and clutched at the table to steady herself. As though from a great way off, she heard Edward's voice, sharp with shock, say incredulously:

"You cannot be serious!"

"Do you suppose, Mr Eastly, that I would jest about such a thing?"

"No, of course not! I did not mean that, but could you not be mistaken? Who in the name of Heaven would do so vile a thing?"

"Hawkesworth!" Lady Tarrington's voice was harsh with a variety of emotions, but above all, with an unshakable conviction. "Jason Hawkesworth! Who else is evil enough to commit such a crime?"

"My lady!" Dr Meredith's voice was very stern. "I realise that this has been a terrible shock to you, but you have no right to make such an accusation."

"No right?" Her ladyship's face was ashen, the pale eyes blazing with anger which to Perdita seemed scarcely sane. "Do not talk to me of my rights! My grandson came near to death tonight, and if that were deliberately done there is only one man in this neighborhood who can possibly be responsible. One man alone wicked enough to plot a child's murder."

"Jason Hawkesworth, my lady, is incapable of so foul a crime!"

"He is capable of any crime, and will go to any lengths to satisfy his hatred," she retorted implacably. "Oh, I know that you do not believe it! You have always taken his part! But one day, Owen Meredith, you will be obliged to face the truth about your precious godson, and if my influence still counts for anything, that day will be soon!"

"My dear ma'am, pray try to compose yourself," Edward said anxiously. "Let us, at least, endeavour to find out how and why the thing could have been done, if done it were." He looked at the doctor. "Are you absolutely certain, sir, that Stephen's illness could have had no natural cause?"

"I wish, Mr Eastly, that I were not certain," Meredith replied grimly. "As to 'how', the poison was undoubtedly contained in the sweetmeats the boy had eaten." He turned to Perdita. "Can you tell me, ma'am, whether anyone else sampled them?"

"I do not think so!" Perdita, still leaning against the

table, tried to speak steadily. "I certainly did not, and neither did the children in my presence, though perhaps Miss Tarrington . . ."

"Melissa does not like sugar-plums," Edward put in. "I know that is so, because I gave some to Stephen when he was confined to bed after the accident last spring, and she would not touch them."

"The accident!" Lady Tarrington looked up; her voice was bitter. "That, too, was Hawkesworth's doing! He is determined that Stephen shall die."

Perdita, glancing at the doctor, saw that he was with difficulty controlling his anger. His voice was rough with it as he said, ignoring the old lady's remark: "Do you know, Miss Frayne, how the sweetmeats came into Sir Stephen's possession?"

She shook her head. "They were among his birthday gifts, but I do not know who sent them. Perhaps Gwenny could tell you that, for she brought the packages into the schoolroom." She glanced at Lady Tarrington. "Shall I ring for her?"

The old lady nodded; Dr Meredith said quietly: "Perhaps you would also be good enough, ma'am, to fetch the box from Sir Stephen's room? Mrs Price is sitting with him at present."

Perdita was glad of the excuse to escape for a few moments from that room where the very air seemed charged with hatred and suspicion, and in the corridor leaned for a second or two against the wall, covering her face with her hands. Could it possibly be true? Were Lady Tarrington's accusations founded upon anything firmer than the obsessive hatred with which she regarded Jason Hawkesworth? Dr Meredith, who appeared to be a man of sound common sense, clearly did not believe so, and there was a crumb of comfort in that thought.

When she returned to the schoolroom, Gwenny was already there. Dr Meredith indicated the box which Perdita was carrying.

"Have you ever seen that before, Gwenny?"

"Aye, sir, to be sure! It be one o' Sir Stephen's presents, the one as I couldn't account for."

"Could not account for?" Lady Tarrington's voice was sharp. "Explain yourself, girl!"

Gwenny looked frightened. "Your ladyship told me to bring all the presents down from the big cupboard on the upper landing in time for breakfast, but there was too many to carry at once. I fetched some, and went back for the rest, and when I come back, that 'un was on the table yonder wi' the others. I thought Miss Melissa or Miss Frayne had put 'un there, or that your ladyship had sent someone along with 'un." She looked anxiously from one to the other. "Did I do wrong, my lady?"

"You were not to know it! You may go!" Lady Tarrington waved her away, barely waiting until the door had closed behind her before saying bitterly to Dr Meredith: "What more proof do you need? Hawkesworth's Indian servant was in my gardens yesterday morning."

"Mahdu here?" Meredith said incredulously. "Surely you are mistaken, ma'am!"

"There is no mistake. I saw him myself," Edward said quietly. "So, too, did two of the gardeners. That would have been, I imagine, about the time that Gwenny was bringing down the presents."

"And Stephen was out early with his dog," Lady

Tarrington added, "so the door at the foot of the spiral staircase was unlocked."

"But neither Mr Hawkesworth nor his servant could possibly have known that!" Perdita spoke impetuously, uttering the thought even as it entered her mind. "Even if your suspicions were correct, ma'am, the whole plan would depend upon the chance of being able to enter the house unobserved, and would need, too, an accurate knowledge of which room to approach."

Three pairs of eyes turned instantly towards her. In the doctor's, she saw surprise and curiosity; in Edward's, warning; in Lady Tarrington's, astonishment, which quickly gave way to anger.

"Your opinion, Miss Frayne, was not sought," she said tartly. "No doubt the man would have effected an entry somehow, had he not been fortunate enough to find the door unbarred, and knowledge of the interior of the house is easy enough to obtain, and will be as long as servants have tongues." She turned again to Meredith. "It is impossible to argue against the facts. An attempt to murder my grandson has been made, and everything indicates that Hawkesworth is responsible. Since Sir Charles Redfall is the nearest magistrate, I shall send for him and place the whole matter in his hands. That scoundrel must and shall be brought to justice!"

For a moment the doctor studied her without speaking. Her voice had been calm enough, cold and level as it always was, but there was a hectic patch of colour on each usually pallid cheek, and her eyes burned fanatically. Meredith sighed.

"My lady, I know that you are as firmly convinced of Jason's guilt as I am of his innocence," he said wearily, "and no amount of argument is likely to alter that. May I suggest that you endeavour to rest now? I shall remain with the boy until he wakes, so you need have no qualms on his behalf."

She looked at him as though about to make some angry retort, but apparently the wisdom of his advice was borne in upon her almost against her will. With an effort which in itself was a clear indication of her exhaustion, she got to her feet. Edward, helping her to rise, said gently:

"Lean on me, dear ma'am! I will help you to your room."

She nodded, and without another glance at Meredith, went out leaning heavily on his arm. Dr Meredith looked at Perdita.

"You must rest, too, Miss Frayne," he said kindly. "There is nothing more that you can do at present."

A dozen frightened questions were spinning dizzily through her tired mind, but she could not find the words with which to ask them. She moved her hands in a little, helpless gesture, and went slowly from the room.

Lying again upon her bed, unable to sleep in spite of her weariness, she tried to grasp the enormity of what had happened. Someone had tried to kill Stephen. That was the one, monstrous fact which loomed like a rock out of the surging currents of suspicion and conjecture, but even now it was almost impossible to believe it.

The feeling of unreality persisted throughout the day. The whole household seemed stunned, shocked into horrified disbelief, yet with rumours seething below the surface, for everyone, down to the youngest stable-lad, now knew that an attempt had been made on the little master's life. Perdita suspected that Gwenny was the source of the spate of gossip, for the girl wore an air of self-importance, and was only too eager to relate any new development.

It was from Gwenny that Perdita learned, early in the afternoon, of the arrival of Sir Charles Redfall, and so when she was summoned to Lady Tarrington's sitting-room, she was not altogether unprepared for the ordeal awaiting her. At the magistrate's request she recounted the story of the sugar-plums, and answered his questions to the best of her ability, but could not find the courage to tell him of her conviction that Hawkesworth and his servant were being unjustly accused. She had fully intended to do so, but in Lady Tarrington's presence her resolution faltered, and though she despised her own cowardice, she could think only that her livelihood depended on not antagonising the old lady.

So she said no more than was required of her, and then went back to the schoolroom not knowing how much credence the magistrate was prepared to give Lady Tarrington's accusations. The afternoon dragged by. Stephen slept for most of the day, watched over continuously by one or other of the female servants, and Dr Meredith, visiting him again towards evening, pronounced himself satisfied.

Melissa was tired after her disturbed night, and subdued by her brother's illness, for though everyone was careful to keep from her any suggestion of foul play, she realised that he was very ill indeed. Perdita found her unusually submissive, even when her grandmother sent word that she was not to come to the drawing-room that evening.

She went early to bed, and Perdita settled herself by

the schoolroom fire with some sewing which would occupy her hands if not her thoughts. She was irked by a
sense of total isolation. Except for the sleeping children, and Gwenny keeping vigil in Stephen's room, she
was completely cut off from the rest of the household.
The schoolroom wing might as well have been a sepa-
rate building, for it could be entered from the main
part of the house only by way of the massive door at
one end of the corridor, while the great thickness of the
ancient walls effectively deadened all sound. Children
might play there without disturbing their elders, or run
out into the gardens down the spiral stair, and this was
no doubt the reason why the old wing had been chosen
for their quarters, but after the events of the previous
night Perdita found its silence and loneliness nerve-
racking.

The light of the fire, and of the branch of candles
beside her, flickered over the time-blackened panelling,
and there was no sound but the wind sighing in the
trees, and the scratching of a mouse somewhere in the
wainscot. The door at the foot of the spiral stair was
securely barred—Perdita herself had shot the heavy
bolts into place when she and Melissa came in from
their afternoon walk—but she still felt tense and on
edge, starting at any sudden sound, and straining her
ears to identify it.

So when she heard a quiet footstep in the corridor,
and the latch of the door lifted, she sat bolt upright,
staring towards it with painful intensity. She relaxed
with a sigh of relief as Edward came in, but her appre-
hensive attitude had not been lost upon him, and when
he had inquired after Stephen, he said with a smile:

"May I bear you company for a little while, Miss

Frayne? It can profit neither of us to brood in solitude over what has taken place."

"Indeed it cannot," she agreed thankfully. "I shall be very glad of your company, sir, for I confess that I find myself in an absurdly nervous frame of mind tonight."

"Scarcely absurd, ma'am," he protested, sitting down on the opposite side of the fireplace. "After last night's shocking events it is not to be wondered at that your nerves are overset." He glanced humorously around the room. "Nor are these surroundings conducive to a happier frame of mind."

She smiled faintly. "No, but I have hitherto accepted them quite happily, and they have not, after all, been altered by what has happened. It is my own thoughts and feelings which make them seem oppressive to-night." She hesitated, nervously smoothing the sewing which now lay folded in her lap. "Mr Eastly, are you at liberty to tell me what has happened as a result of Sir Charles Redfall's visit?"

"Very little has happened, Miss Frayne! When Sir Charles had completed his inquiries here, he went to Mays Court to question the Indian. The fellow swears he never left the house yesterday morning, and Hawkesworth confirms his story. That was to be expected, of course!"

"But you, sir, do not believe it?"

"Most certainly I do not! Did I not see the man myself, not a quarter of a mile from here? He is obviously lying, and so is Hawkesworth, to protect them both."

"But what of the other servants at Mays Court?"

"They say they know nothing. It seems that Mahdu is Hawkesworth's body-servant, and has his quarters in a small room adjacent to his master's. He could have left the house, and returned to it, unobserved by any of them, but none of them are local people, and Hawkesworth has the means to buy their silence if need be. He is fabulously wealthy—though I'll wager the means by which he amassed his riches would not bear close scrutiny."

Perdita flashed him a quick, startled glance, for he sounded now as Lady Tarrington did when she spoke of Jason Hawkesworth. It was perhaps natural that he should share the opinion of his benefactress, yet Perdita felt slightly repelled by his tone. It seemed almost to hold a note of malice. She had been about to disclose her own views on the matter, but now she changed her mind.

"What, then, will happen, Mr Eastly?"

He shrugged. "What can happen? Sir Charles does not feel that there is sufficient evidence to connect Hawkesworth with the crime, since even Mahdu's presence near the house does not prove that he entered it. One can appreciate Redfall's dilemma, but Lady Tarrington is bitterly disappointed and angry that those responsible for the outrage cannot be brought to book."

With difficulty Perdita refrained from pointing out that no one knew with certainty who was responsible, for it was plain that by Edward, as well as by Lady Tarrington, Jason had been judged and condemned even before the magistrate's arrival. Instead, she passed to another matter which had been perplexing her.

"Her ladyship spoke of an accident to Sir Stephen in which Mr Hawkesworth was somehow involved. May I know what she meant?"

"By all means, ma'am! There is nothing secret about it," Edward replied easily. "It happened last March, while Melissa and Stephen were out riding with me. We were on our way to the village, and had just reached the spot at the foot of the hill where the two roads meet when I heard horses coming fast along the valley road. Melissa is somewhat nervous on horseback, so I grasped her horse's bridle, and at the same time called to Stephen, who was a little ahead of us, to stop. I shall never be quite certain whether he deliberately disregarded me, or whether he was unable to control his pony, but whichever it was, a moment later he was in the middle of the road, directly in the path of Hawkesworth's curricle-and-four. In the resultant confusion the pony bolted, and Stephen was thrown."

Pedita was frowning. "Surely that was pure accident! It cannot be compared to what happened last night."

"Oh, there was never any suggestion, even from Lady Tarrington, that it was anything *but* an accident, though it naturally embittered her even more towards Hawkesworth. In fact, had he not handled his horses magnificently, the boy would have been killed. As it was, he suffered a broken arm and sundry minor hurts." He paused, and then added reflectively: "In one way, of course, Hawkesworth *was* to blame. It is madness, criminal madness, to drive on these roads such a team as he had in hand that day, especially at the wicked pace he always seems to favor."

Perdita nodded reluctantly. She had seen such turnouts in London, the light, two-wheeled curricules with their teams of blood-horses, driven by sporting men of fashion, but it was one thing to tool such a carriage round the Park, or along a good turnpike road, and quite another to drive it in these narrow, winding lanes with their high banks and sudden, steep inclines. It was, she reflected with exasperation, exactly the sort of reckless, uncaring conduct one might expect from Jason Hawkesworth.

"I am sure you are right, Mr Eastly, and yet I still cannot understand why her ladyship should believe that accident to have any bearing on last night's shocking events. That scarcely seems logical."

Edward was silent for a moment, frowning a little, and then he said carefully: "You may perhaps have noticed, ma'am, that where Hawkesworth is concerned, Lady Tarrington is governed by emotion rather than by logic, though in this instance I think I can follow her train of thought. Stephen survived the accident, but it may have put into Hawkesworth's mind the idea of contriving a situation which he would *not* survive."

"You cannot mean that!" Perdita made no attempt to disguise her horror. "Besides, you said just now that Stephen's life was saved by Mr Hawkesworth's handling of his horses!"

He shrugged. "One naturally seeks to avoid an accident. It is an involuntary reaction, quicker than thought, but I have no doubt that, if Hawkesworth had been given time to deliberate, the affair would have ended very differently. One thing, at least, is certain. If Stephen's injuries had proved fatal, Jason Hawkesworth would have felt satisfaction, not remorse."

"But this is to regard him as a monster!" Perdita sprang up from her chair and went to stand by the table, her back half turned towards Edward. Her voice was trembling. "I wish I could understand why he is regarded with such hostility! I realise that he is in no

way an admirable person, but surely that is not sufficient reason to judge him guilty of attempted child-
murder!"

Edward had risen also. He bent to pick up the sewing which she had let fall, saying quietly as he placed it
on the table:

"That is something, Miss Frayne, which I could not
explain to you without a great deal of awkwardness,
and though there are those who *could* do so, I advise
you most strongly not to seek such explanations. I can
appreciate your feelings! Knowing nothing of the circumstances, you assume that Hawkesworth is being accused simply because he is unpopular, and that is naturally abhorrent to you. Will you not take my word that
it goes a great deal deeper than that? I assure you that
I would not subscribe to such a suspicion without due
cause."

"I believe that, sir," she replied with difficulty, "and
yet . . ."

"If Lady Tarrington wished you to know the story,
she would tell you," he interrupted quietly. "She may
yet do so, but until she does, Miss Frayne, I counsel
you most strongly, for your own sake, to ask no questions. She will tolerate no sympathy towards Hawkesworth from anyone in her household."

Perdita knew that this advice was good, and resolved
to abide by it, though the questions she dared not ask
continued to plague her. Her belief that Jason had been
falsely accused remained unshakable; she marshalled
several facts in support of it, and tried to ignore an
inner certainty that she would still have believed it
without them. For one thing, at least, she could be

profoundly thankful. She had told nobody of her encounter with him, and it seemed no one else was aware that he had been on Tarrington Chase that day.

Stephen was very ill for several days, but after that his recovery was rapid, since for so delicate-looking a child he possessed remarkable resilience. To everyone's relief, he had no suspicion that his illness had been caused by anything but his own disobedience and greediness, and solemnly informed Perdita that he would never eat sugar-plums again.

Everyone else, however, with the exception of his sister, knew the truth, and no one had any hesitation at all in laying the blame on Jason Hawkesworth. Gwenny, returning from her weekly visit to her family, told Perdita that there was much ill-feeling against him in the village, especially since he appeared to be utterly indifferent to the accusations made against him, and to the resentment they aroused.

Perdita herself could find no peace of mind. She kept the door at the foot of the spiral stair securely barred, going down at frequent intervals to make sure that it remained so, and even when Stephen was well enough to do without anyone with him during the night, she could not sleep for more than an hour or two without getting up and going quietly into his room to assure herself that all was well. She was plagued by doubts and fears which she could confide to no one at Tarrington Chase, and began to look so pale and tired that Dr Meredith, after one of his visits to Stephen, said kindly to her:

"You know, ma'am, it will profit no one, the boy least of all, if you wear yourself to a shadow over what has happened. You were in no way to blame."

"No, I do not think I was," she replied seriously. "I have thought about it a great deal, and I can find nothing with which to reproach myself. It is the future which worries me, not what is past. Sir Stephen is in my care, and if any more harm befell him it would be very much my responsibility."

The doctor gave her a shrewd, questioning glance. "Have you any reason, ma'am, to fear that it might?"

She hesitated, glancing about her. They were standing in the corridor outside Stephen's room, and they were quite alone, for Melissa was in the schoolroom and could not possibly hear what was being said. Perdita returned Meredith's look with a faintly challenging one.

"Sir, one attempt has already been made upon his life, but no real effort has been made to find out who was responsible. That is what frightens me."

"Everyone here at Tarrington Chase, and in the village, will tell you that Jason Hawkesworth is responsible," Meredith replied bluntly. "He has already been tried and condemned."

She made an impatient movement. "I cannot believe that is anything but blind prejudice! Only consider for a moment! If one did plan such a crime, one would hardly entrust the errand to so conspicuous a figure as an Indian servant dressed in the garments of his native land, and that in broad daylight. It would be excessively stupid, and Mr Hawkesworth does not give the impression of being a stupid man."

"No, Miss Frayne," Meredith agreed dryly, "he is not stupid. But he is arrogant and bitter, and since his return to Tarrington has deliberately done everything in his power to anger and outrage the people who live here. They expect the worst of him, and so are ready to believe it."

Perdita would have liked to know why Hawkesworth had left Tarrington in the first place, and why, if he so despised the inhabitants, he had ever returned there, but she shrank from questioning the doctor in case he told Jason she had been asking about him. She could well imagine the sardonic amusement that would provoke.

"You are right, of course," Meredith was saying, "when you speak of blind prejudice, though it needs a stranger to perceive it. I confess that I share your fears. Such prejudice is always dangerous, and on this occasion, particularly so."

"From what I have heard of Mr. Hawkesworth's conduct," Perdita retorted with some asperity, "it would seem that the thought of such danger weighs little with him."

The doctor acknowledged the truth of this with a faint smile, but said gravely: "The danger does not threaten only Jason, Miss Frayne! Whoever made the attempt upon Stephen's life did so with the intention of casting the blame upon Jason, and this they have successfully done. Therefore, if a second attempt were made, and succeeded, the real culprit would have little to fear, for no one would look farther than Mays Court for the murderer. That is the danger, both to Jason and the boy."

VI

Perdita had no doubt that Dr. Meredith's fears were justified, for it seemed quite likely that whoever had made the unsuccessful attempt on Stephen's life would try again. The threat hanging over the child filled her with such foreboding that she even found sufficient courage to speak of it to Lady Tarrington, but this provoked only another bitter denunciation of Hawkesworth, repeated warnings of instant dismissal if she allowed Stephen to have any contact with him, and a point-blank refusal even to consider the possibility that anyone else might have been responsible.

So Perdita was obliged to take what precautions she could on her own account, though she was painfully conscious of their inadequacy. While Stephen's illness

confined him to the house it was comparatively easy to
keep watch over him, but by the middle of September
he was well enough to go out, and it was almost impossible, without disclosing the reason for it, to put any
curb on the freedom he had previously enjoyed. Lady
Tarrington insisted that he was to know nothing of his
danger, and though Perdita agreed with this in princi-
ple, it made her own task doubly difficult. He was a
venturesome little boy, and inclined to be resentful of
what he considered her attempts to mollycoddle him.

She had enlisted Gwenny's aid in keeping an eye on
him, and early one morning the girl roused her with the
information that he had gone out, to take Russet for a
walk in the woods. Gwenny had tried to dissuade him,
then, failing in that, had had sense enough to watch
which way he went, and had seen him set off towards
the Lower Wood, where Bryn Morgan lived.

Perdita rose and dressed as quickly as she could.
There was no time to waste if she were to catch up with
Stephen, so she did not stop to dress her hair, leaving it
in its long braid over one shoulder and tucking it out of
sight under the hood of her thick cloak. Then she went
softly along the corridor and down the spiral stair,
hoping that Melissa would not discover her absence
and start asking awkward questions.

It was a beautiful morning, crisp and bright, the
trees beginning to show the rich tints of autumn. House
and gardens lay bathed in sunlight, but as Perdita hurried down the Long Walk, which sloped gently between
fantastically clipped yew trees to command, at its far
end, a broad view of river and village, she saw that in
the valley a white mist lay so thickly that the hills
beyond seemed to rise from a pearly sea. The country-

side below was blotted out as completely as though it did not exist, and the effect was at once beautiful and strangely eerie, as though Tarrington Chase were an island cut off from all contact with the rest of the world.

At the end of the Long Walk a flight of broad, shallow steps led down to lawns and shrubberies, and through these Perdita hastened towards the gate which opened on to meadow land. Once out of sight of the house she made no attempt to disguise her anxiety, but, alternately walking and running, hurried as fast as she could across the meadow, where cattle swung their heads to watch her with mild, curious eyes.

By the time she reached the woods she was hot and breathless, and had loosened her cloak and pushed the hood back on to her shoulders. She knew which path led to Bryn Morgan's cottage, for Stephen had pointed it out and tried to coax her into taking him there, but she had no idea how far away it was.

The path wandered along the wooded hillside, at times clearly marked, but more often scarcely discernible among rocks and writhing tree-roots, and all Perdita's attention was required to follow it without mishap. As it descended towards the river she found herself entering the mist, which drifted like smoke among the trees and grew thicker the lower she went, until branches and boulders loomed through it in strange, distorted shapes, and everything was beaded with moisture. In its soft, smothering grip the woods were a weird and lonely place, but Perdita's anxiety for the child left no room in her mind for other fears.

She was beginning to wonder whether she had mistaken the way when suddenly a dog began to bark somewhere ahead, and a few minutes later she emerged into a small, open space among the trees, and saw, through the wreathing mist, the squat bulk of a small, stone-built cottage. The dog, a lean, rough-coated lurcher, was tied to a tree-stump a few yards from the cottage door, straining at its chain and barking ferociously, but as Perdita warily approached she heard also, from within the house, a shriller yelping which she thought she recognised as Russet's.

Giving the lurcher a wide berth, she reached the cottage door and knocked upon it with more assurance than she felt. A shouted command from within made the dogs fall silent; the latch lifted, the door swung open, and Perdita recoiled with a stifled cry, for instead of the old poacher, she was confronted by the tall, turbaned figure of the Indian servant.

Shock deprived her of speech, and she stood staring up at the impassive, bearded face until with a scamper of paws Russet came bounding past the man to hurl himself joyously against her, and there was a burst of pent-up, childish laughter from the dim interior of the cottage.

"Oh, poor Miss Frayne! That did give you a fright!" Stephen exclaimed. "But there's no need to be afraid of Mahdu, you know! He is my friend!"

"That is the truth, memsahib," the Indian said gravely, in excellent English. "The little one has nothing to fear from me."

He stepped aside, bowing with his hands before him, palms together, and Perdita went quickly past him to where Stephen was sitting on a wooden stool by the fire. Bryn Morgan stood nearby, but she paid no heed to him as she laid her hand on the little boy's shoulder.

"You must come home at once, Sir Stephen," she

said firmly. "You had no right to come here without permission."

"But if I had asked leave to come, ma'am, you would not have given it," Stephen pointed out reasonably. "Oh, please can we not stay a little longer? Mahdu was just going to tell me how they hunt tigers in India!"

"Let the boy stay!" another voice cut in unexpectedly. "If your conscience pricks you, you can always regard Mahdu's tales as a geography lesson!"

Perdita gasped and swung round, the colour rushing into her face. Jason was leaning with folded arms against the wall, but in the shadows of the low-pitched little room she had been unaware of his presence until he spoke. Bewildered, and vaguely uneasy, she looked from one man to the other, and almost without realising it, moved protectively closer to Stephen. Jason grinned.

"No need to behave like a hen with one chick! The boy is safer here with us than he is in his own home. I thought you knew that." He moved away from the wall and came towards her, bending his head a little to avoid the massive beams supporting the ceiling. "Besides, I want to talk to you. We'll go outside."

Perdita had no intention of allowing herself to be separated from Stephen, but somehow she had no choice in the matter. Jason took her by the arm, and though there was nothing in the least rough or violent about the grip, she found herself compelled to go with him towards the door. Mahdu opened it, and they passed through into the misty stillness beyond. As they began to walk across the clearing, she said bitterly:

"I wish you would tell me, Mr Hawkesworth, what I have done to make you bear such a grudge against me!"

She had the satisfaction of knowing that she had startled him. He halted and looked down at her in blank inquiry.

"Now what the devil do you mean by that? I bear you no grudge!"

"No? Yet you seem determined to cause me to lose my livelihood! If Lady Tarrington knew that you had been anywhere near Sir Stephen, she would turn me out of her house on the spot."

They walked on again. Jason had recovered from his surprise, and said with some amusement: "If she does, come straight to Mays Court. I undertake to see that you suffer no hardship on my account. Does that reassure you?"

She thought it best to ignore this. "Will you be good enough to tell me, sir," she said coldly, "why Sir Stephen is at the cottage yonder?"

He shrugged. "He came there quite by chance, to see Bryn. I can understand that. Bryn Morgan held the same fascination for me when I was ten years old."

"And I suppose that you and your servant are also here 'quite by chance'?" Perdita said scathingly. "What a remarkable coincidence!"

"Don't try to be sarcastic, Miss Frayne! It doesn't become you," he replied calmly. "I've no objection to telling you why we are here. Ever since that attempt on young Stephen's life I have had Bryn keeping watch for any suspicious occurrence which may take place, but it suits me better to come here to discuss the matter with him than for him to come to me. Mahdu accompanies me because I trust him as myself. Are you satisfied?"

"I do not understand," she said slowly, "why you are so concerned about Stephen."

"I am far more concerned about myself," he replied frankly. "Whoever tried to kill the boy sought, with some success, to cast suspicion on me, and I'm damned if I'm going to be the scapegoat for someone else's crime! It is as much in my own interest as in Stephen's to do all I can to protect him."

"Then you believe, sir, that another attempt will be made?"

His brows lifted. "Don't you?"

"Yes," she said in a low voice. "Yes, I do! That is why I followed him in such haste this morning, for in these woods anything could happen to him. Lady Tarrington insists—quite rightly, I think—that he be told nothing of the threat which hangs over him, and he may very easily walk unknowingly into danger. If only her ladyship would take steps to find out who made the attempt on his life, I would be easier in my mind."

"*I* have every intention of finding out," Jason said grimly, "and you can help me, if you will!"

"Is that why you want to talk to me?"

He smiled. "That is one reason, Miss Frayne! Owen Meredith told me you do not share the general belief in my guilt, so I decided to seek your help. As a member of the household, you are in a position to observe things that I cannot. An ally within Tarrington Chase itself is something I did not expect and for which I am duly grateful, even if your belief in my innocence is based solely on the conviction that I possess greater cunning than the murder plot suggests!"

They had reached the edge of the wood by this time, and Perdita halted and stood looking gravely up into her companion's face. The mordant note had crept into his voice again with the latter words, and his hard glance met hers with a touch of derision.

"You are wrong," she said slowly. "I believe that you might quite easily kill a *man,* in anger or to avenge a wrong, but I cannot believe that you would coldly and deliberately plan to murder an innocent child."

She was amazed at her own boldness, and waited apprehensively for an outburst of anger or of savage mockery, but neither came. A look of surprise flashed into the tawny eyes, and he said with a wry smile:

"You read my character with some accuracy, but you will find no one in Tarrington, except Owen Meredith or Bryn, who will agree with you, so for your own sake you would do well to keep that opinion to yourself. But I thank you for it."

"Dr Meredith says that only a stranger can see the prejudice against you which exists in this place," Perdita said reflectively, "and that in such prejudice lies danger, both to you and to Sir Stephen. I will help you if I can, though I do not yet see how."

"Chiefly by keeping watch for any suspicious occurrence within the house, as Bryn is watching outside. Especially for anything which may suggest how the poisoned sweetmeats came to be there, or who the supposed Mahdu really was."

Perdita leaned her shoulders against the tree beneath

which they were standing, and looked up at him with a faint frown. "The supposed Mahdu?"

"Three people say they saw him that morning, yet none of them, as far as I can discover, saw his face. They did not need to! The clothes he was wearing were enough to convince them of his identity, and to implicate both him and me in the plot."

"I have no idea who it could have been," Perdita said doubtfully, "but I have wondered whether one of the servants could have been bribed or tricked into putting the box of sugar-plums among the other presents, and is now too frightened to confess. I cannot imagine why the magistrate did not question them more closely."

"My dear Miss Frayne," Jason said ironically, "do you suppose that Lady Tarrington would ever accept the suggestion that one of her servants could be in league with *me*? You must know as well as I do that, in her eyes, no one but me is capable of this atrocity?"

"In her ladyship's eyes, perhaps, but do you mean to tell me that Sir Charles Redfall is equally prejudiced?"

"Sir Charles Redfall," he replied in a dry tone, "is prepared to believe me guilty for the very good reason that he can think of no one else who might have the slightest motive for killing Stephen. Think for a moment! At ten years old, one can scarcely have made any mortal enemies. The only person who would profit by his death is his sister, who would then inherit the estate, but though Melissa Tarrington is, by all accounts, a sly, spiteful little minx, I think we can absolve her of any desire to murder her brother."

"And you, Mr Hawkesworth?" Perdita asked quietly. "What reason are you supposed to have for desiring the death of a little boy who has done you no harm, and is even inclined to admire you?"

He looked down at her with the expression of savage mockery which made his dark face so forbidding, and Perdita was reminded again of a hawk, a fierce, merciless bird of prey. That, no doubt, was how the villagers saw him, and he seemed to find a kind of satisfaction in fostering the ruthless image, and in doing everything he could to make himself feared and hated.

"Revenge, Miss Frayne!" he was saying now. "Young Stephen is probably the only living being for whom Lady Tarrington has any real affection, so what more effective method of injuring her could I find than by destroying him?"

"Pray do not be absurd!" she said crossly. "I realise that you and Lady Tarrington dislike each other extremely, but it is ridiculous to suppose . . ."

" 'Dislike each other extremely'," he repeated impatiently. "You are not in the schoolroom now, so do not trouble to use polite euphemisms. That old harridan hates me as bitterly as I hate her, and God knows we both have reason enough—thanks to Sir Humphrey Tarrington!"

Perdita looked at him in bewilderment. "You mean her ladyship's late husband?"

"I do!" He paused briefly, and then, his hard gaze holding hers so compellingly that she felt powerless to look away, he added abruptly: "He was my father!"

She continued to stare at him, too startled to be shocked or embarrassed by the implications of his words, but exasperated by her own obtuseness. She ought to have guessed the truth. His eyes, of that curious golden-brown like Stephen's, and like the eyes in the Tarrington family portraits, had told her that there must be a relationship, but for some reason it had never occurred to her that this might be of a left-handed kind.

"Why do you tell me this?" she asked at length in a low voice.

"Because no one else is likely to! It is not a subject considered fit for discussion with a refined young woman, especially an unmarried one! But I have no regard whatsoever for propriety, and if you are to help me, I do not intend you to do so without being aware of all the facts. If, knowing them, you wish to withdraw your offer, I shall not hold it against you."

"But you would despise me for it," she said shrewdly, "for that would prove me guilty of the sort of prejudice I have just been deploring in others. I do not think I shall go back on my word."

"No," he said reflectively, "I don't believe you would!" He was silent for a moment, thoughtfully studying her face, and then he went on more briskly: "I have no doubt you have already seen my mother's grave in the churchyard. Tarrington met her in Bath, where she was employed as companion by some old dowager, and later, following her to London, persuaded her to leave the old lady and live under his protection. At that time he was still a bachelor. He possessed an ancient name, an ancestral estate impoverished by three generations of reckless gamesters, and a certain personal charm. The reason for his visit to Bath was to make the acquaintance of his future wife, an heiress found for him by his uncle and erstwhile guardian."

"And at such a time he had the audacity to pursue

7

a—a less conventional relationship?" Perdita remarked in a shocked voice. "I must say, sir, that Lady Tarrington seems to have had a good deal of provocation."

"She was to have more!" Jason said ironically. "I must explain to you that the proposed marriage was as much a matter of convenience to her as it was to Tarrington, for she was already well past thirty, and singularly lacking in looks and charm. Her father was a respectable tradesman who had suddenly made a great deal of money, so you can imagine that the prospect of becoming Lady Tarrington of Tarrington Chase appealed to her as much as her wealth appealed to her future husband.

"So they were married, and came home to the Chase, and very shortly after that Tarrington brought my mother here and established her at Church House, on the other side of the village. I was born there some four months before her ladyship gave birth to the lawful heir."

He paused, but this time Perdita made no comment. Still leaning against the tree, she stared past him across the misty clearing, remembering the fury in Lady Tarrington's eyes, and a grave under dark yew trees which bore a date only six years past. So they had lived all that time within a mile or two of one another, the wife in the great mansion on the hill, the mistress in the secluded house beyond the church, a house which now stood shuttered and forlorn. How they must have hated each other, and perhaps, in the end, even the man who had brought them into that intolerable situation.

She shivered and drew her cloak more tightly around her. Jason, watching her more closely than she knew, said abruptly:

"Shall I go on, or have I already said enough? Perhaps you now share Lady Tarrington's suspicions of me, and believe her to deserve your undivided loyalty!"

She looked quickly up into his face, reading there the same bitterness which had echoed harshly in his voice, and she felt an unexpected stirring of compassion. She said softly:

"You told me, sir, that I should know all the facts."

He smiled faintly, without amusement. "I told you also that her ladyship had good cause to hate me! She had to watch her husband's bastard son grow up in the village, openly acknowledged by him, just as my mother was openly acknowledged. He made no secret of his preference for me over my half-brother, and that was doubly galling to her because Stephen was a sickly, delicate lad while I was just the opposite. I don't deny that she had her cross to bear, but when the time came, then, by God, she took her revenge!"

Again he paused, and in the silence Perdita was aware of the dripping of moisture from the trees, and the fluttering of a bird among the dying leaves above their heads. The quiet, sad autumn woods seemed a fit setting for the story which was being told.

"My mother," Jason resumed after a moment, "never took more from Tarrington than he could have given her without his wife's money; just enough for us to live very simply, and to pay for my education. From the time I was old enough to understand it, I hated our dubious position in the village, and resented our dependence upon Tarrington. As soon as my schooldays were over, I took myself off to London instead of returning home. For a couple of years I racketed about the town, living in ways more ingenious than respectable, until it became advisable for me to leave England for a while. I had always intended to see something of the world, and meant to stay abroad for a year or two. It was pure chance that the first ship upon which I could find passage was an Indiaman bound for Bombay.

"However, I found India to my liking, and soon perceived the opportunities it offered to a man of enterprise and determination. I remained there for nearly fifteen years, but when at last I returned to England, I was richer than the Tarringtons had ever been. Now, I thought, Sir Humphrey Tarrington should be repaid every penny he had ever given us, and my mother have all the things she could not or would not take from him."

He was silent for a space, and when he spoke again there was no longer anger or mockery in his voice, but only a kind of bitter weariness.

"I had forgotten the changes which can take place in seventeen years! I found that Sir Humphrey Tarrington was dead, as was my half-brother, and the wife he had married during my absence, though two children survived him. The cruellest blow of all was that my mother, too, was dead.

"From Owen Meredith, who had always been our one true friend here, I learned the manner of her death. Tarrington himself had died suddenly, only a few hours after a bad fall from his horse, and he had made no provision for her in his Will. Church House he had bestowed on her for life when he first brought her here, but that was all—after nearly thirty years of selfless devotion such as few wives, even, give to their husbands! With Tarrington dead, and his heir a child still in the nursery, her ladyship's power was absolute, and she used it ruthlessly. My mother was hounded and persecuted until in despair she took her own life!"

The bitter voice ceased at last, and Perdita ventured to steal a glance at his face. She found she could not see it very clearly because of the tears which filled her eyes; tears for him, and for the woman who had been laid in an unmarked grave, and perhaps even for Lady Tarrington herself. Impulsively she put out her hand, but either Jason did not notice the gesture, or he ignored it, and, flushing, she withdrew it.

"What made you decide to live in Tarrington?" she asked curiously. "Surely you must have wished never to see the place again!"

"I, too, wanted revenge," he replied grimly. "It so happened that Mays Court was to be sold. I bought it, though no one here knew who the new owner was until I took possession. Her ladyship had believed that she was rid of the Hawkesworths for ever, but now, whenever she catches sight of my house, she must remember that I am living here, hale and prosperous, while her own son has been ten years underground."

Perdita nodded slowly. She could imagine how the goad of that constant reminder must chafe the old lady's emotions, and keep her hatred of Jason at white heat.

"It is a small enough revenge for what she did to my mother," he added after a moment, "but I give you my word, Miss Frayne, that it is the only revenge I have sought."

"I do not doubt that," she replied in a low voice. "Everything you have told me has simply strengthened my conviction that you had nothing to do with the attempt on Stephen's life." She smiled rather uncertainly. "Perhaps because such cruel and devious plotting seems to me at odds with your temper."

His expression relaxed a little of its grimness. "You consider me more likely to have ridden straight to the Chase and strangled the old witch out of hand? It was a temptation, believe me, but I resisted it! So your promise to help me still holds good?"

"Yes, it does, though even if I do discover anything, I do not know how I am to tell you of it. I would not dare to send you a message."

"Send one instead to Owen Meredith," he suggested, "or give it to Bryn. He has a boat moored below the cottage, and once across the river it is less than a quarter of a mile to my house." He hesitated, looking at her with a faint frown. "You are to take no risks, though! Perhaps, after all, I should not allow you to play any part in so dangerous a game."

"You can scarcely prevent it, sir," she said indignantly, "and pray give me credit for a trifle of common sense! Besides, Sir Stephen is in my care, and I shall naturally do everything I can to ensure that he comes to no harm, and to find out who threatens him."

His expression relaxed still further, and a glimmer of amusement came into his eyes. "Very proper," he remarked. "Exactly the sentiments which one would expect from a conscientious governess!"

"I trust that is what I am," she replied with dignity, "even though it pleases you to make fun of me on that account."

He studied her with increasing amusement. She was still bare-headed, and in the damp air, tendrils of brown hair had come loose from the long braid to curl childishly about her face. Her cheeks were flushed and the green-grey eyes sparkling with indignation.

"How can I help it," he replied frankly, "when you look about sixteen years old, and not in the least like a governess, conscientious or otherwise? I'm damned if I know why I am addressing you with such formality, when I could be calling you 'Perdita'!"

She gasped, staring incredulously at him. "How do you know my name?"

"Young Stephen told me. It seems he saw it inscribed in a book belonging to you. You may remember I told you I would discover it if I chose."

She did remember, and also the circumstances in which the words had been spoken. It seemed to her that the situation was becoming dangerously similar, and, now thoroughly flustered, she said indignantly:

"You may have discovered my name, sir, in this underhanded fashion, but I have not given you leave to use it! Now I must fetch Sir Stephen, for if we are absent too long, questions will be asked, and that would doubtless be as little to your liking as to mine."

"Running away again?" he said ironically. "So you are afraid of me on your own account, if not on Stephen's!"

"I am not afraid of you," she replied crossly, "but you have no notion of proper behaviour, and I find that exceedingly distasteful. It is not at all what I have been accustomed to."

"You will soon get used to it," Jason said reassuringly. "It is Miss Frayne, not Perdita, who finds it shocking."

She looked uncertainly at him, and then, completely at a loss, brushed past him and walked quickly back to the cottage. Opening the door, she said briskly:

"Come, Sir Stephen! We must go now!"

Stephen obeyed the command resignedly, apparently realising it was useless to plead for further delay. He took reluctant leave of Bryn Morgan and Mahdu, and then of Jason, who had followed Perdita at a more leisurely pace. Perdita herself was determined that she would not even glance at Hawkesworth again, but as she turned towards the path leading to ~~the top of the~~ hill, he laid his hand briefly on her arm and said in a low voice:

"Remember, Perdita! Take care!"

She did look up at him then, and saw that he was now completely serious. She nodded without speaking, and followed Stephen and Russet along the path, reflecting that Jason Hawkesworth was the strangest man she had ever met. A man who, on his own admission, had lived by his wits, and whose great wealth had probably been amassed in disreputable ways, yet with a curious kind of honesty which would not accept her help until she knew the truth about him. A man with no regard for convention or propriety, who seemed to find amusement in shocking her, and yet could arouse her compassion as readily as her anger. Whom she was prepared to trust when so many distrusted him, and whom, even in the first shock of that morning's encounter, she had known in her heart she was glad to see again.

VII

As they climbed the hill, Stephen chattered so excitedly
of the things Mahdu had told him that Perdita began to
foresee danger in his enthusiasm. When they reached
the edge of the wood, and could see the great house
rising before them beyond meadow and garden, she
stopped and laid a hand on his arm.

"Sir Stephen, there is something I must say to you.
You know, do you not, that your grandmama would be
very angry indeed if she knew in whose company you
have spent the past hour? It was exceedingly wrong of
me to permit you to remain at the cottage, but I know
how eager you have been to talk to Mahdu, and it
seemed to me that if you were allowed to do so just
once, it might content you."

"And you wanted to talk to Mr Hawkesworth," Stephen reminded her innocently.

She gasped, feeling the colour flooding into her face, and gave silent thanks that Jason himself was not present to hear that artless remark. She tried another approach.

"Do you like having me for your governess?"

"Oh yes, indeed I do!" he replied earnestly. "Everything is so much more jolly than it used to be. Miss Caterby was always fussing, and scolding me for being noisy or untidy, and she did not like me to bring Russet into the schoolroom." He broke off, the significance of her question dawning upon him. "You are not going away, are you? Oh, Miss Frayne, please do not!"

"I should go away very quickly indeed if Lady Tarrington found out that you have been with Mr Hawkesworth and his servant," Perdita said ruefully. "I was given strict orders not to allow that under any circumstances, and I have disregarded them. Her ladyship would be fully justified in dismissing me."

"Then we mustn't tell her! We mustn't tell anyone! If anyone asks where we have been, we'll say we took Russet for a walk in the woods. Don't worry, ma'am! I can keep a secret!"

Perdita felt a twinge of remorse for encouraging him to deceive his grandmother, but stifled it with the reflection that it was justified by Lady Tarrington's refusal to suspect anyone but Jason. She herself was the only person close to Stephen who was not blinded by the same unreasoning prejudice, and she dare not take the risk of being sent away. There was another risk, however, which must be guarded against.

"Then this is a secret, my dear, which we will keep

between us, but you must understand one thing. There must be no more jaunts to Bryn Morgan's cottage in the hope of finding Mr Hawkesworth or Mahdu there. I must ask you to promise me that."

He looked crestfallen, but after a little hesitation gave the required promise. Perdita was relieved. No harm had come of that morning's escapade, but if it were repeated, Stephen could well be playing into the hands of his enemy, who would probably be quick to profit by any contact with Hawkesworth. The promise was a safeguard both for Jason and the boy, though Perdita was reluctant to admit to herself that the one seemed as important as the other.

In the days which followed she kept careful watch over Stephen every moment he was in her care, and was constantly alert for anything which might offer a clue to the identity of his enemy. She even asked Nurse a few cautious questions, reasoning that a woman who had been in the family service for more than half a century might well be aware of matters which others did not know or had forgotten. The old woman had taken a liking to Perdita and was always glad to see her, either alone, or accompanying the children on their regular visits, but Perdita found her to be as firmly convinced of Jason's guilt as her mistress was, and even more reluctant to talk about him. So agitated did she become that Perdita hastily changed the subject, and took care not to refer to it again.

October came, crisp and cold, with misty mornings of white frost which gave way, as the day advanced, to sunlight which seemed brighter because of the glowing colours on which it shone, where, crimson and brown and gold, the woodlands burned against green grass and deep blue sky. It was a beautiful autumn, and gradually Perdita came under the spell of the country-side's wild splendour. It seemed less alien now, and, were it not for the grim spectre of attempted murder which haunted Tarrington Chase, she felt that she might have come to love it.

One morning she was awakened by the sound of Stephen's door closing, and then, after a pause, she heard him creep past her own door and down the stairs. She sat up, vaguely disturbed, for though he nearly always took Russet for a run in the gardens before breakfast, there was something unusually stealthy about this morning's departure, while the dimness of the light filtering through her window told her that he was up much earlier than usual.

She got up, shivering as she hurried into her clothes, for on these cold mornings a chill seemed to emanate from the ancient stone walls and floors. Flinging her thick cloak about her, she went quietly out of the house, going first to the outbuilding where Russet was kennelled and finding it, as she had expected, empty. She walked on into the gardens, telling herself that she was being over-anxious, but unable to rid herself of a sense of foreboding.

It was that uneasiness which led her down the Long Walk, where the yew trees were white with frost and festooned with spider webs, every strand of which seemed to be set with tiny jewels. She did not really believe that Stephen would break his promise, and when she came to the top of the steps and saw, on the frost-whitened lawn below, his footprints, accompanied and circled by the paw-marks of the scampering dog, leading straight towards the meadow-gate, her disappointment was as sharp as her dismay.

Angry now, she hurried in the same direction, as she had hurried once before, through garden and meadow and down the precarious path to the Lower Wood. The cottage, when she reached it, was deserted. No dog barked, only the faintest thread of smoke drifted up from the chimney, and her peremptory knocking on the door brought no response.

She walked a few paces from the house and stood looking about her, her breath rising smokily on the still air. Had she misjudged Stephen, and come on a fool's errand? Yet if he had not come to the cottage, where had he gone? He could be anywhere in the spreading acres of woodland which clung, silent and somehow menacing, to the precipitous shoulders of Tarrington Chase.

Then suddenly she heard his voice somewhere in the wood below the cottage, calling Bryn Morgan's name in a puzzled, questioning tone. Perdita hurried round to the back of the house and found another path leading down towards the river.

Following it, she soon caught the flash of water through the trees below her, and a minute or so later found herself close to the broad, swift river, though still some fifteen feet above it. Below, she could see a sturdy rowing-boat drawn up above the water-line, and Stephen standing beside it, while Russet rooted happily in the undergrowth a short distance beyond. From where she stood, still hidden among the trees, the path dropped sharply towards the boat, steep and narrow and precariously poised above the hurrying water.

Hampered as she was by her long skirts, she was afraid to attempt it, even though hand and foothold were offered by a fallen tree, which had apparently plunged down the hillside in some forgotten gale and now lay with its roots firmly entangled in the undergrowth, and its dead branches trailing in the river.

Stephen called again: "Bryn! Bryn Morgan, where are you?"

He moved forward, closer to the river's brink, and Perdita parted her lips to call him back. Then, sudden and sharp, a shot rang out from somewhere on the opposite bank, and her indrawn breath was released instead in a piercing scream as the little boy pitched forward and rolled into the water. The current seized him and swept him into the trailing branches of the fallen tree, where he hung, limp and motionless, held there briefly by his clothing.

Before the echoes of her scream had died away, Perdita had flung off her cloak and was scrambling recklessly down the bank, along the tree's sloping trunk. The icy chill of the water as she entered it took her breath, but she struggled on until her outstretched fingers clutched at the child's jacket, and then somehow she edged her way forward until she could get her arm around him and raise his head and shoulders clear of the water. She had to support both him and herself by her other arm across a sturdy branch, for there was no solid ground beneath her feet.

She could not tell whether Stephen were alive or dead. His eyes were closed in a face the colour of ashes, and blood streaked the sodden, light-brown hair. Nor could she see any way of getting him back on to the high bank, where Russet was running to and fro, yelping and whining. Slight though he was, his weight was too much for her, and her first, convulsive effort to drag him higher caused the tree to give an ominous, downward jerk, as though the unwonted weight at its lower end were dragging it free from its anchorage.

A shout from the far side of the river brought a momentary flash of hope, for two men, labourers by their dress, were running along the bank from the direction of the village. They paused opposite to where Perdita clung desperately to the tree, but they were clearly at a loss, looking frantically this way and that and not knowing what to do.

Then with a drumming of hooves on turf a big roan horse flashed into view from among the scattered clumps of trees farther downstream. Perdita recognised the tall figure in the saddle, and as the horse slid to a halt beside the two villagers, she sent across the water a faint, despairing cry for help.

She saw Jason spring to the ground and say something to the other men as he dragged off coat and boots, and then he was down the bank and into the water. In an agony of hope and fear she watched him, praying that he was a sufficiently powerful swimmer to overcome the fierce, treacherous currents of this wild stream. It seemed an eternity before he reached her, but when he did, and stretched out his hand to help her, she gasped faintly:

"Stephen! Take Stephen!"

He got a firm grip on the boy, easing the aching strain on her tired arms, and said urgently: "Hold on, then, for God's sake! I will come back for you!"

She nodded, and sensed rather than saw him strike out for the far bank. She clasped both arms round the branch to which she clung and let her head sink forward until her cheek rested against the rough bark, for the deadly cold was draining her strength, and the pull of the current like steady, relentless hands seeking to drag her down. She was only half conscious by the time Jason reached her again, and scarcely aware of the grim fight which had to be waged against the turbulent river before he staggered with her at last into shallow water, and the watching men came to aid them both on to the bank.

As she lay on the frosty grass, gasping and choking, the thought of Stephen forced itself through her failing senses. She dragged herself up on to one elbow and saw him lying nearby, wrapped in Jason's discarded riding-coat, the grey pallor of his face emphasised in ghastly fashion by the bright blood that streaked it. Crawling to him on hands and knees, she was fumbling with numbed hands for some sign of life when Jason himself spoke close beside her.

"He is alive!" The words came haltingly between great gasps for breath. "We must get him to shelter." He turned to one of the countrymen. "Take my horse, and ride for Dr Meredith! Send him to Mays Court as quickly as he can come, while you," to the younger of the pair, "go rouse my household! Tell them what has happened and bid them make ready."

The two labourers had been watching him with grudging respect, for they knew that only a very strong man and expert swimmer could have accomplished that double rescue, but they seemed curiously reluctant to obey his orders. Perdita saw them hesitate, exchanging a doubtful, uneasy look.

"Oh, go! Go!" she cried hysterically. "Can you not see the need for haste? The child may be dying!"

Thus urged, they did obey, though not without a backward glance. Jason bent over Perdita again, grasping her arm to raise her to her feet.

"Do you think you can walk to the house?"

She nodded, conscious only of the need to get Stephen where he could be warmed and cared for, and Jason bent again to pick up the unconscious child. From where they stood, they could see Mays Court a few hundred yards away up the gentle slope, but to Perdita the distance seemed to stretch like miles. She stumbled along beside Jason as fast as she could, but her sodden skirts clung hamperingly to her legs, and before they had gone far she tripped and fell. As she struggled to her feet again, he shifted Stephen to his shoulder, holding him there with one hand, and put his other arm around her waist, helping her along.

In this fashion they had covered two-thirds of the distance when they saw Mahdu running fleetly to meet them, asking, as he came within earshot, what sounded like an anxious question in his native tongue. Jason replied in the same language, and handed Stephen over to the servant. The Indian bore the boy swiftly towards the house, while Jason, ignoring Perdita's feeble protest, picked her up and carried her in the same direction.

In the pillared, marble-paved hall of Mays Court, where servants had gathered to stare and whisper, he set her on her feet again and beckoned forward one of the women whose dress indicated that she was a lady's maid.

8

"Take Miss Frayne to your mistress," he said briefly.
"Ask Miss Delamere to look after her." To Perdita he
added reassuringly: "Go with her! The boy will be well
cared for, I promise you."

She had no strength left to protest, or even to reply,
but let the abigail help her up the stairs and so to a
luxuriously appointed dressing-room. As they entered,
the door on the far side opened and Miss Delamere
herself appeared, wrapped in a beribboned cloud of silk
and lace, and with her blonde curls escaping from beneath a becoming cap.

"Lord save us, Lizzie!" she exclaimed drowsily.
"What is going on? Who in the world is this?"

"It's the governess from Tarrington Chase, ma'am,"
Lizzie explained. "There's been an accident! Her and
the young gentleman nigh drowned in the river, by all
accounts."

"The river? At this hour?" Miss Delamere said incredulously, adding, without waiting for a reply: "Well,
no matter for that! You poor thing, you must be chilled
to death! Come to the fire, and Lizzie shall help you
out of those wet clothes."

She led the way into the room from which she had
emerged, a bedchamber as richly furnished as the
dressing-room, where a fire blazed cheerfully. Perdita,
too exhausted to argue, allowed herself to be di-
vested of her sodden garments, wrapped in one of
Miss Delamere's frivolous dressing-robes, and settled in a chair close to the fire while Lizzie dried
her hair.

For the moment, a sense of unreality had taken possession of her. The beautiful room, with its hangings of
silk and brocade, and the rich Eastern carpet covering

the floor; the expensive absurdity of the robe she had been given to wear; the expert attentions of the well-trained abigail, were all so far removed from anything she had ever experienced that she felt as though she had strayed into a different world. As, indeed, she had, she reflected hazily. The world of Perdita Frayne, governess, and that of the rich Mr Hawkesworth's *chère-amie*, were poles apart.

While Lizzie looked after Perdita, Miss Delamere had been moving restlessly about the room, sitting for a minute or two before the dressing-table, then getting up to go to the window and draw the curtain aside to look out at the frosty morning, where pale sunlight was now beginning to dispel the mist. At last she came to stand by the fire, and, looking down at Perdita, asked abruptly:

"*Was* it an accident, ma'am?"

For Perdita, the blunt question completely shattered the illusion of security created by this warm, perfumed room. She shivered violently and shook her head.

"No," she whispered, "it was a deliberate attempt at murder. A shot was fired from this side of the river. Stephen fell into the water and I could not get him out. Had Mr Hawkesworth not chanced to be riding in the park, we should both have drowned."

"He rides there every morning at this unholy hour," Miss Delamere remarked. "I cannot imagine why . . ."

She broke off, and they stared at each other in appalled silence, struck simultaneously by the same thought. If Jason's morning rides were common knowledge, it would soon be decided who had fired the shot.

"But he saved us both, at risk of his own life!" Perdita said desperately after a moment. "Surely no one will believe that it was he who . . . who tried to kill Stephen?"

"The old woman will believe it," Miss Delamere said with conviction, "and if she does, so will the whole village. They follow her like a flock of sheep!" She threw herself into a chair on the other side of the fireplace, pulling off her cap and shaking out her bright curls. "If Hawkesworth shows any sense at all he will leave this place while he may! He ought to have done so when the first attempt on the child was made."

A feeling of panic clutched at Perdita's heart. If Jason went away, to whom could she turn for aid if she discovered the identity of Stephen's enemy? Yet if he did go, perhaps the murderous attempts would cease, since there would no longer be a scapegoat to bear the blame, so what right had she to wish him to stay?

"Can *you* not persuade him, ma'am?" she ventured.

"I?" The other girl laughed, with mingled amusement and exasperation. "My dear, no one can turn Hawkesworth from his chosen course! *I* did not want to live in this God-forsaken valley, but one comes to him on his terms, or not at all. Had I refused to leave London, there were others willing enough to take my place." She paused, regarding Perdita with a hint of friendly mockery in her blue eyes. "I shock you, ma'am, but one must be practical in these matters, and he is very generous."

Perdita had no idea what reply to make to this. Miss Delamere was plainly lost to all sense of shame, but she had been sympathetic and kind and Perdita did not wish to appear ungrateful. She decided that the best thing to do was to change the subject.

"I am so worried about Stephen!" she said anxiously. "May I prevail even further on your kindness, ma'am, by asking you to lend me something to wear? My place is with him."

"Your place, my dear, after what you have been through, is in a warm bed," Miss Delamere replied bluntly. "I will willingly lend you some clothes, but would far rather have a room prepared for you. The child will have every care."

Perdita thanked her, but insisted that it was her duty to go to Stephen, so Miss Delamere told Lizzie to fetch some suitable clothes. These did not fit very well, since Perdita was taller than the other girl and built on less generous lines, but the style and quality of them added to her feeling of unreality, for she had never worn such garments in her life. The abigail coiled up her hair, now drying into unruly waves, in a simple knot on the crown of her head, and then led the way downstairs again.

Perdita followed slowly, exasperated to discover how weak and shaken she felt. From time to time she still shivered violently with cold, though it was a chill which sprang as much from her gnawing anxiety about Stephen as from anything else. She could not get out of her mind the memory of him as she had last seen him, inert in Mahdu's arms, his face as livid as death and blood and water dripping from his hair.

In the hall, a footman greeted them with the information that Dr Meredith was with Sir Stephen, and that Mr Hawkesworth was waiting in the library for the doctor to join him. He then ushered Perdita firmly into the library also, giving her no chance to protest.

Jason was standing by the fire, leaning one arm on the mantelpiece as he stared down into the flames, but when Perdita was announced he looked up with a frown and then came quickly across the room. He was immaculately dressed, and only the damp waves of his thick black hair betrayed that anything unusual had befallen him.

"What the devil are you doing down here?" he greeted her. "I told them to make a room ready for you, and intended to send Owen Meredith to you when he has attended to the boy."

"Miss Delamere advised me to go to bed, but I could not! I had to find out how Stephen is. I wanted to go to him." She broke off, staring up at him with dilated eyes, trembling with suddenly sharpened fear. "Mr Hawkesworth, you did not lie to me? He *is* alive?"

"I give you my word that he is! You shall see him as soon as Owen will allow it." He took her hand in a strong, warm clasp, adding with mild exasperation: "You ridiculous girl, you are still half frozen! Come and sit down."

She allowed him to lead her to a sofa before the fire, and sat there trying to control the tremors which continued to shake her. Jason looked at her for a moment and then went across to a table which stood between the tall windows, returning with a glass in his hand.

"Drink this," he said quietly.

Perdita eyed the golden liquid with some misgiving. "What is it?"

"Brandy," he replied laconically, then, when she shook her head, he sat down beside her and, taking her hand again, clasped her fingers firmly about the glass. "Do as I bid you! I have already found this morning eventful enough without being obliged to deal with a swooning female."

She uttered a choking sound between a laugh and a sob, and sipped obediently at the brandy. It made her gasp and grimace, but he insisted that she should drink it all, and after a little she felt a warmth stealing over her and the violent trembling lessened.

"That's better!" Jason took the empty glass from her and put it down. "I am still of the opinion that you should be in bed, but since you refuse to behave in a sensible manner, perhaps you will tell me exactly what happened this morning. Why were you and young Stephen on the river bank at that hour?"

She explained how she had heard Stephen go out, and followed him. "I cannot understand why he went to the cottage," she added in a troubled voice. "I had made him promise me that he would not, and it is not like him to break his word. He plainly expected to find Morgan there, for I heard him calling his name just before the shot was fired."

Jason was frowning. "Could *you* have been seen from this side of the river?"

"No, for I was still up on the bank, where the path from the cottage reaches that fallen tree. Only Stephen was in clear view, down by the boat. It must have seemed that he was quite alone."

"Which is exactly what our unknown marksman expected," Jason said grimly. He saw the sudden, frightened question in her eyes, and added quietly: "Whoever fired that shot was not there by chance! He must have found some way of enticing the boy to that particular spot, and to what, but for you, would have been certain death."

VIII

Perdita stared at him, her mind fighting against the truth of what he said. Yet she had known it all along, from the moment the murderous shot rang out. Hearing it put into words simply lent it an added horror.

"But how?" she whispered. "How could he have been persuaded?"

"The boy may tell us that when he recovers," Jason said thoughtfully. "Whoever lured him there did not expect him to survive, and so may not have troubled to cover his tracks as far as Stephen is concerned. That may prove to be his one mistake, for otherwise the trap was cunningly set, both for Stephen and for me. It was obviously known that I ride in the park every morning, and there were even witnesses provided in the shape of these two fellows from the village. They have been working on repairs to the boundary wall on the far side of the park, and walk there each day along the river bank."

Perdita shuddered, the horror of what had happened flooding over her again. Poisoned sweets among a child's birthday gifts; a little boy lured blindly into a murderous ambush; and on each occasion the stage set to convict an innocent man. The utter callousness and uncanny knowledge of the would-be assassin were terrifying. There seemed no defence against him.

She realised that she was trembling again, and gripped her hands tightly together, staring at a tiger-skin rug on the floor at her feet. Then she thought how excited Stephen would have been by this impressive trophy of the hunt, with its beautifully striped fur and great, savage head with snarling jaws, and tears suddenly blurred her vision. She rose quickly to her feet, turning her head away and pressing her fingers to her eyes.

"It is so horrible!" she said in a breaking voice. "To try deliberately and cold-bloodedly to murder a ten-year-old child! How can anyone be so inhuman?"

Jason had risen when she did. He did not speak, but he put his handkerchief into her hand and then took her by the shoulders and pulled her gently to him. For a little while she sobbed weakly in his arms, her head against his chest, and when at length she regained command of herself and drew away, it was not from any belated sense of decorum, but because she had become aware of the perilous sense of comfort and reassurance she derived from being there.

"Forgive me!" she said unsteadily. "I am being intolerably foolish, though I assure you I am not usually so poor-spirited." She tried to smile. "I am sure that a weeping female is almost as tiresome as a swooning one."

"It would be a very remarkable female who was not overwrought by the experience you endured this morning," he replied. "I am an unthinking brute for causing you to dwell upon it!"

"No," she said in a low voice. "We must talk of it now, for this may be our only opportunity." She sat down again on the sofa and resolutely dried her eyes. "I promise you I will not lose command of myself again, and we *must* try to think of some clue to the author of these dreadful events. Did you see nothing suspicious, sir, during your ride?"

He did not reply at once, but stood looking down at her with a curious expression. "You are a remarkably brave woman, Perdita Frayne!" he said quietly. "No, I saw nothing. I heard the shot, and your scream, and rode immediately in that direction. The marksman was probably concealed in one of the clumps of trees near the water, but if he was I passed without noticing him. I have sent Mahdu to search along the river bank, but no doubt it is a fool's errand. The bird will have flown long since."

"And I have no notion from which direction the shot came, except that it was from this side of the river," she said despondently. "Everything happened so quickly." She hesitated, twisting the handkerchief between her hands. "Mr Hawkesworth, has it occurred to you that the best way to ensure Stephen's safety, and your own, may be for you to leave Tarrington? Whoever has been trying to kill him seems determined to cast the blame upon you." She paused, but when he did not immediately reply, added defensively: "Miss Delamere said much the same thing just now."

"Alicia's chief concern is to return to the gaiety of London," he replied dryly, sitting down again beside her. "I have no intention of leaving Tarrington—but before you condemn me as an obstinate fool, consider one thing. If I went, and the attempts on the child's life ceased, what would that be taken to prove? Not my innocence, I'll lay odds! Lady Tarrington would say— and the whole parish would agree with her—that it was conclusive proof of my guilt! No, there is only one answer, and that is to find the real culprit."

"But how?" Perdita asked despairingly. "We have not the least idea where to look, or when he may strike again, or even why he does so at all. One might as well try to grasp a handful of mist!"

"It was something a damned sight more solid than mist which fired that shot this morning," Jason replied grimly. "This is not a ghost we are dealing with, my dear, but a mortal being with some pressing reason for wishing young Stephen out of the way. If we could discover the reason, it would be only a short step to discovering the man himself. It is the seeming lack of purpose in the crime which is so incomprehensible."

"I suppose," she said hesitantly, "that Stephen *is* the prime victim, and not you? I know it sounds improbable, but if you had some enemy who was afraid to move openly against you, might he not attack you in this way?"

"In the hope of seeing me hang for Stephen's murder? He would need to be extraordinarily ruthless, and though I have made more than one enemy in the past, I don't think any of them could be in Tarrington without my knowledge. Besides, what need for so elaborate a scheme? It would be far simpler to put a bullet in my back from the sort of ambush used this morning."

The picture these words conjured up was so vivid and horrible that Perdita made a little, shuddering gesture of protest. There was silence for a moment, and then Jason went on:

"Nor can I believe that anyone who bears me a grudge fears me so much that he would go to such lengths to avoid confronting me. It is not everyone, my dear Perdita, who regards me with the apprehension that you do!"

She looked quickly at him as he sat, half turned towards her, one arm resting along the back of the sofa. "But I do not . . ." she began, and then, seeing the expression in his eyes, broke off to add reproachfully: "How can you jest, at such a time?"

"I would rather jest, inappropriate though it may be, than allow you to brood any longer over what has happened," he replied. "You must try to put it out of your mind."

"I do not think I shall ever be able to do that," Perdita said in a low voice. "To come so close to death is an experience not readily forgotten. Nor do I forget, sir, to whom I owe my life, and if I have not yet expressed my gratitude, it is because I can find no words which seem adequate."

"In some parts of the world," he remarked, "the belief is held that if a man saves a life, that life belongs to him thereafter. What a pity it is not so in England!"

His tone was quizzical, and so was the glance still resting upon her face. Perdita coloured faintly.

"I think you are teasing me, Mr Hawkesworth, and though no doubt you do so with the praiseworthy intention of diverting my mind, I assure you that it is not in the least necessary. I shall not disgrace myself, nor embarrass you, by breaking down again."

"My intentions are seldom praiseworthy," he replied with some amusement, "and I cannot resist teasing you, Perdita, because it throws you into such enchanting confusion."

She knew that this was true. No conversation she had with him ever followed a predictable course, and she frequently, as now, had no idea what answer to make. She ought to rebuke him for using her name so freely, but, apart from the fact that at the present time this would seem ungracious, she felt certain that he would pay no heed.

It did not seem to matter very much. She was beginning to feel a little light-headed, the combined effect of the warmth of the fire and of the brandy he had made her drink; a not unpleasant detachment which, while doing nothing to detract from her awareness of the morning's grim events, was enabling her to remember them more calmly. Dr Meredith coming into the library at that moment, it even enabled her to listen with a degree of composure to what he had to tell.

"Stephen is an exceedingly fortunate little boy," Meredith said seriously. "By a miracle, the shot inflicted no serious injury, though had it struck him only an inch lower, he would have been instantly killed. He regained consciousness for a few minutes while I was dressing the wound, and recognised me immediately.

My chief concern is the effect upon him of cold and shock, though we must hope that a few days of rest and quiet and careful nursing will be sufficient to counteract that." He glanced at Hawkesworth. "Jason, Lady Tarrington must be informed."

"I have already sent word. It seemed best to forestall any hue and cry when Perdita and the boy were found to be missing."

Meredith nodded, and went to sit in a chair near the fire. He looked tired, and had obviously been called from bed by Jason's summons, for he had not had time to shave.

"This is a shocking affair," he said. "I still do not know exactly what happened, and if it will not distress Miss Frayne too much, I shall be glad to hear all the facts."

Briefly, Jason recounted them, while Perdita sat gazing into the fire and picturing the commotion which must have been caused at the Chase when the news arrived. No doubt Lady Tarrington would come to Stephen as quickly as she could, and though Perdita knew she had nothing with which to reproach herself, she felt a sudden pang of misgiving. Too much had happened that morning to make the thought of confronting her ladyship anything but daunting.

She had hardly been listening to what the two men were saying, until her attention was caught by Jason saying with a touch of bitterness:

"Good God, Owen, of course I shall be accused! Even those fellows who were there almost refused to leave me with the boy!"

She remembered then how unwillingly the two villagers had obeyed his command to go and raise the alarm. She had not realised the significance of it at the time, but now it was only too clear.

"How can they be such fools?" she exclaimed with angry distress. "Surely they cannot believe that you would risk your life to save Stephen if you *had* fired that shot?"

"They will find some villainous reason to account for it," he replied contemptuously. "You have heard the old saying about giving a dog a bad name! I have had such a name in Tarrington these five-and-twenty years."

"Not entirely undeserved in the first instance," Owen commented dryly. "There is also a proverb about sins coming home to roost."

"You have it wrong, my dear Owen!" Jason retorted savagely. "Curses come home to roost! The sins of the fathers are visited upon the children!"

He got up abruptly and went across to the window, where he stood staring out, his hands gripped hard together behind him. Perdita saw Meredith frown and bite his lip as though reproaching himself for his own tactlessness, and then, as she looked across at the rigid figure by the window, she was aware of a sudden and almost overmastering desire to go to Jason and comfort him. Shaken by the force of that unexpected emotion, she sat staring at his broad, unheeding back and wondering whether this feeling, too, were an effect of that unaccustomed glass of brandy. She must be intoxicated, she thought wildly, to entertain such feelings, or to presume that any comfort she could offer would be either needed or acceptable.

For a minute or two there was silence, and then Jason remarked in his normal tone: "Lady Tarrington

has wasted no time! I can see her carriage coming
along the avenue." He turned to face the room again,
and Perdita saw that though a sardonic smile touched
his lips, his eyes remained hard. "I'll wager that is
something which, until this morning, not one of us ever
expected to see!"

There seemed to be no reply to make to this. They
heard the carriage wheels crunch on the gravel in front
of the house, and the snorting and stamping of horses,
and then a peremptory knocking on the front door.
Jason strolled unhurriedly across the library and into
the hall, and Dr Meredith followed him. After a brief
hesitation, Perdita got up and tiptoed across to the
door. Opening it a crack, she peeped cautiously out.

Her view of the hall was restricted, but she saw
Jason go forward to greet the newcomer, and then
Lady Tarrington came in sight. In spite of the haste
with which she must have set out, she was elegantly
and fastidiously dressed, and only the livid pallor of her
face betrayed her feelings. She looked implacably at
Jason, making no response to his coldly courteous
greeting, and then turned to the doctor.

"How is my grandson, Dr Meredith? Take me to
him immediately."

With a quick, warning glance at Jason, Owen
stepped forward to escort her upstairs, speaking reassuringly of Stephen's condition. Jason watched them
cross the hall, and then turned to the library again. He
had betrayed no resentment at that deliberate affront,
but when he came into the room Perdita could see the
smouldering anger in his eyes.

She had moved only a little way from the door, but
he seemed for the moment to have forgotten her pres-

ence. He walked across to the table where the silver
tray bearing decanter and glasses stood, and poured
some brandy. He drank it with a quick, angry gesture,
and then looked up to meet Perdita's troubled gaze.
Immediately his expression relaxed a little, and he gave
a twisted grin.

"Confound the woman! I've allowed her to annoy
me, and that is something I swore she should never do.
All the provocation was to be upon my side."

"I do not wonder that you are angry," Perdita said
indignantly. "To treat you so, when she is a guest in
your house and under so great an obligation to you! It
is unforgivable!"

"It's an obligation which she finds intolerable," he
pointed out. "That, and the fact that circumstances
make it necessary for her to enter my house at all. I'd
be willing to wager that by the time she comes downstairs she will have convinced herself that she owes me
nothing, and that Stephen is alive at this moment only
to serve some more sinister design than the one which
failed this morning."

Perdita sighed. She thought that what Jason said was
probably true, though she could not imagine by what
mental process her ladyship would arrive at that con-
clusion. There was a brief pause, and then he said, in a
tone of contempt:

"What can have become of the ubiquitous Mr Eastly? I imagined that in this sort of crisis he would not be
far from the old lady's side."

"He left early yesterday morning to visit his family
in Staffordshire," she explained. "I understand he had
received word that his father is ailing." She regarded
Jason curiously. "Why do you dislike him?"

9

He shrugged. "I do not know him, but I have a strong dislike of all smooth-tongued young men who batten on foolish women. Have you ever known a tutor who behaved as he does, or was so treated by his employer?"

She agreed that she had not, but in justice to Edward felt obliged to explain that his father and Lady Tarrington were life-long friends.

"And Eastly was quick to profit from that! You may depend that he is feathering his nest very comfortably while he is at Tarrington Chase." Jason paused, and then added reflectively: "He must have found it easy to win her favour. He looks not unlike her own son."

This had never before occurred to Perdita, but now, remembering the portrait of the elder Stephen Tarrington, she realised that it was true. Was that the reason for the old lady's affection for Edward, and had he perceived it and turned it to his own advantage, as Jason suggested?

The door opened and Mahdu came silently into the room. He bowed low to Perdita, but addressed Jason.

"Nothing, sahib! There are signs that someone lay hidden among the willows opposite to where the boat is kept, and that a horse has been tethered beyond the park, but that is all."

"And that much we had already guessed," Jason said grimly, "so it tells us nothing. The fellow must be miles away by now—or, more probably, going about his lawful business under our very noses!"

Perdita shivered, for the thought that the would-be murderer was someone known to them was a horrifying one. Yet it was more likely than not, for neither attempt on Stephen's life could have been made by a stranger.

The sound of footsteps in the hall, and the voices of Lady Tarrington and the doctor, made her turn towards the door with an agitation she could not subdue. They came into the room, and her ladyship, ignoring Jason, walked straight across to Perdita.

"I am under a great obligation to you, Miss Frayne," she said in her cold, level voice. "This is the second occasion on which Stephen has owed his life to you. I am taking him home immediately, and I have no doubt that you will be thankful to return also. This has been a most disagreeable experience for you."

"My lady," Dr Meredith said forcibly, "I cannot too strongly advise you against moving the boy at this time! He should remain where he is until tomorrow at least. Preferably for several days."

"I cannot agree," she replied. "The journey is a short one, my carriage is well sprung, and I have come amply provided with blankets and pillows. I intend to convey my grandson to his own home."

"It is unwise and unnecessary!" Meredith said angrily. "I must warn you, ma'am, that I will not be responsible for any harm which may come to the child as a result of it."

"You need not, Dr Meredith! I have been responsible for Stephen since the day of his birth, and *I* will decide what is best for him."

"There is no need to move the child!" Jason spoke curtly, almost with contempt. "He is welcome to remain here as long as Dr Meredith considers it necessary, and you, ma'am, are at liberty to stay with him if you wish."

"Remain here?" She turned on him as furiously as though he had offered her an intolerable insult. "Do you imagine I would have set foot in your house at all but for the urgent need to take my grandson out of it? I will have him at Tarrington Chase, among those I can trust, and not here at your mercy!"

"How can you say such a thing?" The words broke from Perdita's lips before she could check them; her voice was shaking with anger. "Do you not realise that I could never have saved Stephen unaided? He owes his life to Mr Hawkesworth, not to me!"

She was aware of Jason's quick, startled glance, and of the astonished anger in Lady Tarrington's eyes, and was mutinously glad that she had spoken. After a moment of amazed silence, her ladyship said coldly:

"You are impertinent, Miss Frayne! I repeat that I am in *your* debt, but do not impose too far upon my gratitude. You are overwrought at present, and so I will ignore what you have just said. Now be good enough to come with me."

She turned towards the door. Jason opened it for her, looking down at her from his great height with a contempt which he did not try to disguise, and which robbed his harsh, dark face of every vestige of kindness or humour.

"The boy has suffered no harm from me," he said in a voice which matched his look. "If I strike at an enemy, I strike true, and I have no quarrel with a child who was still in the nursery when my mother killed herself."

Lady Tarrington paused for an instant, and Perdita saw in her eyes a curious blend of hatred and alarm. Then she went past Jason into the hall, and began to give instructions for Stephen to be brought down to the carriage.

Jason said something quietly to Mahdu, and the Indian bowed and moved away. Perdita, who had reluctantly followed Lady Tarrington from the library, said in a low voice to the doctor:

"Is there a very grave risk, sir, in moving Stephen in this way?"

"It is extremely unwise," he replied grimly, "but we must hope that no harm will result from it. I shall follow you to the Chase, and see how he is after the journey. I have given him medicine which should make him sleep for several hours, so we must hope that it will not cause him too much distress."

Stephen, wrapped in blankets, was carried downstairs by the footman who had come in attendance upon Lady Tarrington, and the old lady and her personal maid, who had been waiting in the carriage, fussed about, settling him among the pillows. Dr Meredith had joined them, and Perdita was left standing with Jason in the hall.

Mahdu reappeared, carrying over his arm a pelisse of dark-blue velvet, trimmed and warmly lined with fur. Jason took it from him and held it for Perdita to put on, but she looked with dismay at the richness of it, and murmured a protest.

"Don't be absurd!" he said impatiently. "You cannot go out into the cold without a wrap. Put it on!"

Reluctantly she turned and slipped her arms into the costly garment. His hands on her shoulders turned her gently to face him again, and he said softly:

"Don't try to defend me, Perdita! I'm grateful to

you, but it does no good and will only make your own situation intolerable."

She looked up into his face. He was still holding her, and for one crazy instant she thought he was going to kiss her, as he had done that day at the Spur. Then Dr Meredith's voice spoke from the front door.

"Lady Tarrington is waiting for you, Miss Frayne!"

She gave a gasp of dismay, and then with a whispered farewell broke away and hurried across the hall. At the door she paused for an instant to look back at him, and then ran down the steps and climbed into the carriage.

Jason strolled across to join Meredith, and they stood under the pillared portico, waiting for the doctor's gig to be brought round, and watching the carriage going slowly away under the elm trees. Owen bestowed a shrewd, thoughtful glance on the younger man from beneath grizzled brows.

"A remarkable young woman, that little governess!" he said casually. "Not many girls possess the courage and resourcefulness she showed today. Most of 'em would have swooned or had hysterics when the child was shot."

"Perhaps it would have been better for Perdita if she had done so," Jason replied, and met the doctor's startled look with one of grim meaning. "Twice now she has thwarted a murderous design against the boy. Do you suppose that anyone as ruthless as this would-be killer will tolerate such interference in his plans for much longer? She is in a danger that she does not even recognise. I *must* find out who is behind the affair, but the damnable thing, Owen, is that I still have not the least idea how to do it!"

IX

"Only to think, miss," Gwenny remarked in a tone which blended genuine concern with a kind of morbid relish, "if you hadn't went after Sir Stephen this morning, the poor little soul wouldn't be alive this minute. No one in Tarrington'll ever forget that, look!"

"And if Mr Hawkesworth had not risked his life to rescue us, both Sir Stephen and I would have drowned," Perdita reminded her. "I hope that no one will ever forget that."

"Him had his own reasons for doing it, no doubt!" Gwenny said darkly. "Who's to say what be in his wicked mind? Folk won't forget, mind, that 'twas him shot the little lad! It be as well her ladyship fetched you

both from there, or there's no telling what might have
happened to you."

Perdita sighed, but did not pursue the argument. She
felt too weary, for though on their arrival at Tarrington
Chase that morning Dr Meredith had ordered her to
bed, and given her medicine which had made her sleep
for most of the day, she had not yet fully recovered
from her ordeal. She was still in bed, and Gwenny,
having brought her a meal, was now engaged in packing the clothes borrowed from Miss Delamere. Her
ladyship, it seemed, had announced that Miss Frayne
would wish to return these without delay, and had ordered Gwenny to see to it. Perdita was not surprised.
Lady Tarrington's disgust at seeing her grandchildren's
governess in those elegant, expensive garments had
been very plain.

She wrote a brief, civil note of thanks to Alicia Delamere, and sent Gwenny off with it, and the parcel,
thankful to be rid of the girl's disturbing chatter. Yet
even when left alone with her thoughts she could find
no peace, for these followed a course the folly of which
she well knew. Her fears for Stephen were sharper than
ever, yet, insensibly, it was Jason's safety which had
come to mean most to her. The trap had been set for
him as well as for the child, and if Stephen had fallen
victim to it, in the present temper of the village Jason
would have had little hope of escape.

Lying there in her cheerless, sombre room, watching
the leaves drift from the trees in the October dusk,
Perdita faced the fact that she was in love with Jason
Hawkesworth. It seemed absurd after their few, brief
meetings, yet she knew it to be true, and the knowledge
filled her with dismay. Like every girl, she had dreamed

of falling in love, though she had never had any very clear picture in her mind of the man who would capture her heart. Well, now she knew, and little happiness it was likely to bring her. It was almost impossible to envisage Jason settling down to marriage, and any less permanent relationship would be out of the question. All she could hope for was to keep her feelings hidden, and so emerge from the affair with her pride and dignity, if not her heart, still intact.

She got up next morning at her usual time, feeling quite certain that Lady Tarrington would expect it. Stephen, she was glad to hear, was a good deal better, and it seemed that no harm had resulted from moving him from Mays Court. When Perdita went in to see him, she found him more concerned about Russet than about his own injury. Bryn Morgan had found the little dog roaming in the woods and brought him home, but though Stephen had been told of this, he would not rest until Perdita fetched Russet from his kennel and carried him into his young master's room, promising to make the dog her special responsibility until Stephen was well again.

About mid-day, Dr Meredith looked into the schoolroom. He had been with Stephen, and now wished to assure himself that Perdita had completely recovered. When he had assured her and her pupil that he was satisfied with Stephen's progress, he said kindly to Melissa:

"If you would like to spend a little while with your brother, my dear, I think he will be glad to see you now, if Miss Frayne will give you leave. Not more than ten minutes, and do not allow him to become excited."

Perdita gave her consent at once and Melissa hurried

away, for in spite of their frequent squabbles, she and Stephen were deeply attached to one another; a result, perhaps, of their solitary childhood. When she had gone, Owen said, with a searching look at Perdita:

"And what about you, my dear young lady? You are still looking decidedly peaked."

"Thank you, I am perfectly recovered now, except that I still feel a little tired," she replied. "I am glad to have a moment alone with you, sir! Pray, what is the reaction in Tarrington to yesterday's events?"

"Precisely what Jason prophesied!" Meredith replied grimly. "No one is prepared to give him any credit for saving you and the boy, being convinced that it was all part of some dark though inexplicable plot. I tell you, Miss Frayne, I have lived and worked among these people for forty years, and count many of them my friends, but today I would gladly consign them all to perdition!"

"I do not understand how they can be so blind!" Perdita said in a tone of distress. "I know that Mr Hawkesworth has done a good deal to antagonise them, but this bitterness against him seems out of all proportion."

"I will tell you one reason for it, ma'am," Owen said bluntly. "Fear! They are afraid of Jason because he knows that not one of them lifted a finger to help his mother when Lady Tarrington was hounding her to her death!" He nodded grimly in answer to Perdita's startled, almost disbelieving look. "I am not exaggerating, Miss Frayne! From the time Sir Humphrey died, her ladyship persecuted that unfortunate woman in every way that vindictiveness could devise and wealth and influence achieve. And the people of Tarrington, who

had been Susan Hawkesworth's neighbours for thirty
years, and were well aware that she had done more to
influence Sir Humphrey for their good than his wife
had ever tried to do, were afraid to go against her
wishes. They are all involved in the guilt of Susan's
death."

"I did not realise that," Perdita said in a low voice.
"Mr Hawkesworth did tell me something of the sort,
but I thought he was influenced by his natural bitterness, and perhaps a little by remorse for having left his
mother so long without news of him."

Dr Meredith shook his head. "It is perfectly true! It
was as though Lady Tarrington's hatred of Susan had
been dammed up through all the years of her husband's
lifetime, and that his death opened the flood-gates.
Now that hatred has transferred itself to Jason."

Perdita shivered. "Yes, I know! I have seen it, and it
seems to me that in that respect her ladyship is scarcely
sane. It is a dreadful thing, and the most dreadful
aspect of it is that by her blind obsession against Mr
Hawkesworth she is endangering Stephen's life. I have
tried and tried to think of a way to persuade her that
the danger lies elsewhere, but the only person she
might attend to is Mr Eastly, and he, I fear, is as firmly
convinced of Mr Hawkesworth's guilt as Lady Tarrington herself."

"I dare say he finds it prudent to agree with her,"
Owen replied scornfully. "No, ma'am, nothing will
convince Lady Tarrington, and you would be most unwise to attempt it. And that puts me in mind of a message which Jason charged me to deliver to you."

Perdita was dismayed to find herself blushing, and
hoped devoutly that Dr Meredith would not observe it.

If he did, he gave no sign, but went on in the same tone:

"He is very much concerned that you may arouse Lady Tarrington's anger to such an extent that she dismisses you, and he wishes me to tell you that if that should happen, you are to depend upon him for any assistance you may need."

There was a pause, while Perdita became needlessly busy with the lesson books scattered on the table, and when at length she replied, she made this an excuse not to look at the doctor.

"Mr Hawkesworth is most kind, but already I stand too deeply in his debt. Even if Lady Tarrington dismissed me today, I have been in her employment for two months, and in justice she could not turn me off without paying my coach-fare back to London. I have relations there, a cousin with whom I lived after my father died."

"A cousin," she thought bitterly as she spoke, "who will never forgive me for leaving her house, and who would turn me away if I came to her door barefoot." But no one in Tarrington knew that, and to be entirely alone and friendless would be preferable to seeking charity from Jason.

In her agitation she was unaware that her companion was regarding her with a good deal more comprehension than she could comfortably have sustained had she been conscious of it. Owen Meredith had not spent a lifetime ministering to his fellow beings without becoming acutely perceptive, and he had little difficulty in correctly divining Perdita's feelings.

"Without wishing to add to your anxieties, ma'am," he said dryly, "I fear I cannot share your faith in her

ladyship's sense of justice. If she finds that you take
Jason's part, she is quite capable of turning you out-
of-doors without a penny, and without a reference. If
you should find yourself in that awkward predicament,
I hope very much that you will come to me for assistance, since you are naturally reluctant to accept Jason's offer of help. No awkwardness need attach to
your accepting aid from an old man like me."

"Except that I have not the slightest claim upon
you," she said unsteadily. "You are very good, Dr
Meredith! I do not know why you should be in the
least concerned about me."

He smiled. "My dear young lady, I am extremely
fond of that godson of mine, and you have refused to
be influenced by the prejudice against him, even though
it would be in your own interest. I respect courage and
honesty, and would not wish anyone to suffer on account of those qualities if I could prevent it."

"I do not think I have very much courage," Perdita
replied in a wry tone, "for the thought of this unknown
enemy terrifies me. It is like trying to come to grips
with a shadow. A shadow existing on its own, with no
solid substance behind it." She looked at Meredith with
a faint frown in her eyes. "Do you think it possible, sir,
that old Nurse may know something? When I first came
here, she said something to me which might have been
a warning. That evil begets evil, and that there had
been a shadow over this house for many years."

"She was probably referring to Sir Humphrey's association with Susan Hawkesworth," Owen replied.
"Nurse is a strict, God-fearing woman, and though she
was devoted to Tarrington she never forgave him for
keeping Susan here in the village, or for his undisguised

preference for Jason over his lawful son. Stephen was a timid, delicate lad and his father despised him for it, while though Jason was a wild young rip, there is no doubt that Tarrington wished he were the heir."

"I suppose you are right, sir," Perdita said with a sigh. "Yet if she, who has served the family for over fifty years, can tell us nothing, who can?"

The return of Melissa prevented Dr Meredith from offering any answer to this, and a minute or two later he took his leave. That was the only opportunity Perdita had to talk privately with him, for on his subsequent visits she saw him only briefly, and never alone. She was therefore obliged to depend upon Gwenny, that avid collector of gossip, for news of what was happening in the village.

This was anything but reassuring. Mahdu, riding through Tarrington, had been violently abused, and the other servants at Mays Court—none of them local people—now refused to stir beyond the boundaries of their employer's property. Jason himself still rode abroad as arrogantly as ever, but he had let it be known that he went armed, and would not hesitate to defend himself if the need arose. This served only to increase the violence of feeling against him, and so the vicious circle went on.

At Tarrington Chase, gloom and foreboding possessed the whole household, for though Stephen was recovering, everyone was afraid that another attempt on his life might be made once he was up and about again. Lady Tarrington was more irascible than ever, so that even Melissa had begun to dread the nightly visit to the drawing-room, while to Perdita it had become an ordeal which overshadowed the entire day.

On the fourth evening after her and Stephen's narrow escape, she was alone in the schoolroom, Melissa having gone to bed, when Edward unexpectedly walked into the room.

"Mr Eastly!" she exclaimed in surprise. "I did not know that you had returned. I trust this means, sir, that your father has recovered?"

"Yes, I thank you. That is to say, he is sufficiently restored to health for my presence to be less necessary at home than it appears to be here." He came across the room and stood looking gravely down at her. "I cannot tell you how excessively shocked I am! Lady Tarrington sent me word of what had happened, but until I talked with her just now I did not realise the full extent of it." He held out his hand. "My dear Miss Frayne, how very much we owe to you, all those of us who are fond of Stephen!"

Perdita put her hand into his, since it seemed ungracious to ignore the gesture, but said firmly: "To Mr Hawkesworth also, sir! Without his aid I could have saved neither Stephen nor myself."

"Ah, yes! Hawkesworth!" Edward repeated in a hard voice. "A cool customer indeed, is he not? I am told he still rides boldly about the parish as though he had not the least thing on his conscience."

"Why should he not, sir?" Perdita retorted sharply. "He performed an act of great heroism, at considerable risk to himself. It is a thing not many men could have accomplished."

"Oh, I will not argue with you, ma'am, on the score of Hawkesworth's physical prowess! If his character were as fine as his physique, he would be a paragon indeed."

Perdita got up from her chair. "Mr Eastly," she said coldly, "I may as well warn you without delay that I will listen to no more empty accusations against Mr Hawkesworth. I never did believe him responsible for the first attempt on Stephen's life, and I would suppose that his rescue of the child made it evident, even to the meanest intelligence, that he certainly had no hand in the second."

"I would say rather that, realising the attempt had failed, he was quick-witted enough to try to divert suspicion from himself by playing the hero."

"That is a despicable thing to say!" Perdita cried angrily. "In any event, the attempt had not failed! He need only have gone quietly away and left the river to do its work—*if* he had desired Stephen's death."

She broke off, conscious that her anger at Edward's gibes had betrayed her into an unwisely spirited defence of Jason. Edward was looking curiously at her.

"It seems that Hawkesworth has one champion at least!" he remarked. "It is natural, I suppose, for you to feel obliged to defend him after he saved your life, but I would advise you, if you wish to remain here, to keep your opinion to yourself."

"I say only what I believe," she resumed more calmly. "I think it foolish and dangerous to cling so blindly to belief in Mr Hawkesworth's guilt. Have you never paused to consider that, by doing so, everyone is playing into the hands of the real criminal?"

Edward leaned against the edge of the table behind him and regarded her with tolerant amusement. "If you will indicate to me, Miss Frayne, who the real criminal may be, I will undertake to alter my opinion of Hawkesworth." He paused inquiringly, but Perdita was silent, biting her lip in vexation at her own inability to reply. Edward smiled. "Precisely! There is no one else with the smallest reason for wishing Stephen out of the way. To be sure, Hawkesworth's motive is so vile that it may well seem incredible to you, but it is the only one which exists."

Perdita turned abruptly away and stood staring down into the fire, knowing that, on the face of it, what Edward said was true. Lack of motive was the blank wall against which all suspicion and conjecture eventually shattered—yet a motive there must be. Someone wanted Stephen dead, and if she continued to spring so fiercely to Jason's defence, she might put that person on his guard and make even more remote the possibility of stumbling on some clue to his identity. Edward's advice was sound. In future she would disguise her feelings, keep a close guard on her tongue, and let it be thought that she shared the general opinion.

Since only Perdita herself, and Stephen, knew of the little boy's promise not to visit Bryn Morgan, it occurred to no one to wonder why he had been on the river bank that morning, for the fascination the old poacher held for him was well known. Perdita wondered about it a great deal, but was reluctant to question him until it was absolutely necessary. No danger was likely to threaten him as long as he was confined to bed.

He reached the fretful stage of his recovery, not yet well enough to be allowed to get up, but sufficiently restored to find being kept in bed irksome. He had not yet resumed his lessons, and the task of keeping him amused taxed the combined ingenuity of Edward, Melissa and Perdita. Lady Tarrington spent a good deal of

time with him, and allowed him to have Russet in his
room for the greater part of the day, but even this
failed to content him. He fretted when the dog was
banished to its kennel at night, while the fact that
Gwenny was sleeping in the little room between his and
Melissa's caused him to complain bitterly that he was
being treated like a baby. He was, in fact, as tiresome a
patient as only a normally active small boy could be.

One night, when the wind moaned round the house
and rustled the ivy cloaking the schoolroom wing, Perdita lay sleepless for hours. It was not merely the keen-
ing of the wind, or the muted roar of it in the nearby
trees, which kept her awake, though these desolate
sounds played their part in the depression which
engulfed her. Gwenny had been to the village that day,
and had returned to announce gleefully that the feeling
against Jason, far from subsiding, seemed to be
stronger than ever before. Perdita's anxiety on his behalf was consequently sharpened, while that evening
she had been further dismayed by a strong hint from
Lady Tarrington that her services would not be required beyond the end of the three months which the
old lady had allowed for her "experiment". Meanwhile,
Perdita could discover no likelihood of seeing Jason
again, except in church on a Sunday, with Alicia Delamere on his arm.

She wept a little, from loneliness and longing, and at
last fell asleep to the dreaded and now frequently re-
curring nightmare of a cold, swift, relentless river, and
a dead tree which dragged itself inexorably from its
precarious anchorage. She woke sobbing, the terror and
despair of the dream still vivid, and for a few bewildered seconds could not identify the commotion which

had roused her. Then she realised that it was Russet's hysterical yelping, coming, inexplicably, from Stephen's room. Obeying the commands of instinct rather than reasoned thought, she sprang out of bed and stumbled, still not fully awake, in the direction of the noise.

Inside the room she almost collided with Gwenny, who had rushed in by way of the connecting door from her own bedchamber. The lamp which during the boy's illness was kept burning low at night on a table in one corner cast a dim, flickering light over the scene, enough to reveal Stephen sitting up in bed, and the curtains billowing in the wind around an open casement, beneath which Russet was leaping and scrabbling against the wall, still uttering his shrill, angry barks.

Both young women rushed across to the bed. Perdita, flinging her arms around Stephen, asked in alarm:

"What is it? What has happened?"

"Someone tried to get in through the window!" Stephen's voice was unsteady, but he seemed more excited than alarmed. "Russet frightened them away before they could! Isn't he a splendid watch-dog, Miss Frayne?"

Perdita ignored for the moment Russet's sterling qualities and the mystery of his presence in the room. "Through the window?" she repeated incredulously. "But it must be a sheer drop of nearly thirty feet!"

"The ivy!" Gwenny said in a shaken voice. " 'Er be that old and thick, look, 'tis as easy as climbing a ladder. Sir Stephen climbed down 'un hisself last summer, but none of us ever thought as someone might climb up. Lord forgive us, the little lad might have been murdered in his bed!"

"Hush, Gwenny!" Perdita spoke sharply, with a

quick, warning glance, as Melissa came running into
the room. Stephen was taking the incident with admirable calm, but his sister could not be depended upon
to do likewise. "Close the window, for pity's sake, before we all take our death of cold, and then turn up the
lamp. Russet, be quiet!"

Somewhat to her surprise, the spaniel obeyed this
command, and began sniffing suspiciously around the
big, carved chest which stood beneath the window.
Gwenny pulled the casement shut and tried unsuccess-
fully to fasten it, saying as she did so:

"The catch be broke! Him must have forced it, the
black villain!"

Perdita paid no heed to this, being fully occupied in
trying to soothe Melissa's alarm, assuring her that the
intruder had fled and was not likely to return. She was
only partially successful, for Stephen's excited interjec-
tions were of no help at all, while the fact that she was
still trembling with shock made it difficult for her to
speak as calmly and reassuringly as she would have
liked. The knowledge that Stephen was not safe even
while asleep in his bed was so horrifying that for the
moment she dared not allow herself to dwell upon it.

Gwenny pulled the curtains and went to turn up the
lamp, almost falling over Russet, who was now growling and pawing at some object which he had scraped
out from the gap between chest and wall. The light
brightened, dispelling the shadows, and Perdita
breathed a sigh of relief to see the room returning to its
normal aspect, giving at least an illusion of security.
Then Gwenny uttered a shriek, and pounced on the
thing at which Russet was pawing.

"God save us, miss, see here! Him must have dropped 'un when the dog went for 'un!"

She came across to the bed, and Perdita sat silent, staring with a feeling of sick dismay at the object which lay across Gwenny's work-roughened palm. A dagger, its long, murderous blade glinting evilly, its hilt wrought in an intricate design which proclaimed, unmistakably, its Indian origin.

X

Had Perdita been alone with Stephen, she would have hidden the dagger and said nothing, trusting the child to keep silent, too; but she was not alone. Gwenny and Melissa had seen the weapon, so now it must be shown to Lady Tarrington, to provide yet another piece of evidence against Jason, for who else in Tarrington was likely to be in possession of an Indian dagger? The other, and more horrifying thought she thrust out of her mind; the thought that if Russet had not been in his young master's room, Stephen would have been found with that dagger in his heart.

It was Melissa who had smuggled the spaniel into her brother's room, by way of the spiral stair, after Stephen had been settled for the night. This fact

emerged later, after Lady Tarrington had been roused
—and if Perdita needed any confirmation of how completely the schoolroom wing was cut off from the rest
of the house, she found it in the circumstance that,
until Gwenny went to fetch her mistress, no one had
been aware of the noise being made there. It was dawn
before any of them got to bed again, and when at last
they did, a stalwart footman was left on watch in Stephen's room.

That afternoon Perdita was summoned to Lady Tarrington's sitting-room, and found Sir Charles Redfall
there. The old lady's face was grey with fatigue and
rigid with anger, while the magistrate looked more
harassed than ever. Perdita expected to be asked for an
account of the previous night's disturbance, but instead
Sir Charles questioned her closely about the earlier attack by the river, an ordeal which, thanks to Dr Meredith, she had been spared at the time. She answered
him frankly, glad of a chance to lay the true facts before him, unbiased by Lady Tarrington's hatred and
prejudice, and when the whole story had been told, he
turned to her ladyship.

"I fear, ma'am, that there is nothing in what Miss
Frayne has told me to prove that Hawkesworth fired
the shot which injured the child. He *may* have done so,
but so may anyone else concealed along the river bank,
while if Hawkesworth was responsible it is in the highest degree unlikely that he would then have risked his
life to undo what he had done."

The old lady looked implacably at him. "I sought
your aid, Sir Charles, in bringing this scoundrel to justice, but you seem concerned only to find excuses for
him! He has tried three times to murder my grandson!

Is he to be allowed to make the attempt again and again until he succeeds?"

"You have no right to say that!" The words broke from Perdita's lips before she could check them, for she could not hear Jason so slandered, and remain silent. "He saved Stephen's life! What more proof do you need that he means him no harm?"

"Do you dare?" Lady Tarrington's voice trembled with anger. "Do you dare, you impudent hussy, to take that tone with me? Upon my soul, I believe you are all in league with the fellow! The evidence of his guilt is before your eyes," she flung out a pointing hand towards the dagger which Redfall had laid on the table, "and you refuse to accept it!"

"Lady Tarrington!" Sir Charles spoke soothingly, with a glance at Perdita which clearly warned her to say no more. "It has been proved beyond question that neither Hawkesworth nor his servant could have been at Tarrington Chase last night. The Indian is unwell and confined to his bed, as Dr Meredith has confirmed, while as for Hawkesworth himself . . ." Sir Charles hesitated and looked again at Perdita, this time with an expression of faintly embarrassed apology. "Miss Delamere can swear that he did not leave the house."

Perdita glanced quickly away, the colour rising in her cheeks, though not, as Sir Charles imagined, because she was embarrassed by the implications of Mr Hawkesworth's alibi. Redfall's words had conjured up in her mind a picture of Alicia's beautiful room, and Jason with her there; she was shaken by a jealousy and pain greater than she would have believed possible, and which she thought must be apparent to her companions.

It seemed that it was not. Lady Tarrington said harshly: "The woman is lying! One of her kind will say or do anything for money. Hawkesworth's kept mistress! A fine witness, upon my soul! What of that dagger? Is there anyone in Tarrington apart from Hawkesworth or his servant likely to own an Indian dagger?"

"I told you, ma'am, what Hawkesworth said when I showed it to him. That it is a piece of valueless trumpery, the sort of weapon he would not have owned even when he was in India, much less have taken the trouble to bring back with him to England. The sort of cheap curio which any seaman might fetch home as a souvenir of his travels."

"There are no seamen in Tarrington," her ladyship replied coldly. "I know every man, woman and child in the parish, except the strangers at Mays Court, and I know that is where you will find the criminal."

It was plain that no argument would convince her otherwise, but it was equally plain that Redfall felt that the evidence against Jason, flimsy enough where the first two attempts were concerned, did not even exist in the third case. Obviously there was no immediate danger of the law being set in motion against him, and Perdita's relief was so great that she felt almost lighthearted.

This happier frame of mind endured for several days, until the next Sunday. With others from the Chase, she went as usual to church—Mrs Price had remained behind in charge of Stephen—and was already in her place when Jason entered, alone. As he strode along the aisle to his pew, Perdita saw that many hostile looks were directed towards him, but it was not until the service was over and the congregation dis-

persing that she was made fully aware of the violence
of feeling against him.

She was already in the churchyard when he emerged
from the church, and stood for a second or two in the
doorway, ironically surveying the scene before him. He
wore what Perdita always thought of as his "hawk
look", and perhaps it was the contempt in his expression, as much as anything else, which roused the anger
of the assembled villagers. Sunday or no, churchyard or
not, there came a sullen muttering, and a slight but un-
mistakable movement, as though the crowd were about
to converge upon the church door. Perdita gave a gasp
of alarm and dismay, and with difficulty conquered an
impulse to run to Jason's side, for the isolation of that
arrogant figure tore at her heart.

For a few moments the situation was tense with im-
pending violence, and then Jason moved unhurriedly
forward. He might have been alone in the churchyard
for all the notice he took of the threatening crowd, and
his very indifference disconcerted them. They looked
sidelong at one another, and no one had the courage to
make the first move. Jason strolled along the path,
through the lych-gate and across the grassy space
beyond to where his horse was tethered, and resentfully
they watched him go, watched him mount and ride
away down the steep slope beneath the chestnut trees.

Perdita drew a long breath of relief. She was trembling, for she had just seen, for the first time in her life,
how anger and suspicion could weld a group of people,
all worthy enough as individuals, into a thing of ugly
and frightening power, and she realised that the law
was not the only, or the most pressing danger which

Jason might have to face. A glance at the Tarrington carriage, in which Lady Tarrington, Melissa and Edward were already seated, showed that the old lady was leaning forward with an expression of malevolent satisfaction, and the suspicion flashed into Perdita's mind that, disappointed of support from the magistrate, her ladyship was using her considerable influence to stir up hatred against Jason.

After the attempt to break into Stephen's room, it was obviously impossible to keep from the children the fact that he was in danger, but as far as Perdita knew, they had never spoken of it to anyone. She was therefore all the more surprised when, as she sat with Stephen one afternoon, he said suddenly:

"Miss Frayne, *I* do not believe that Mr Hawkesworth would do anything to hurt me, do you?"

"Of course he would not, my dear," she replied without hesitation. "Had he wished to do so, he would not have pulled you out of the river when you tumbled in, would he?"

"Mr Hawkesworth pulled me out?" Stephen was staring at her in astonishment. "But Grandmama told me it was you who did so!"

"I certainly went after you, but then I found that I could pull out neither you nor myself. Luckily, Mr Hawkesworth came along. He fetched us both out of the water and took us to his house. Later your Grandmama came and brought us home."

"And I don't remember anything about it!" Stephen mourned. "I wanted so much to go to Mays Court, and when I did get there, I did not know. Oh, it is too bad!"

"You had had a nasty knock on the head," Perdita reminded him. "It is no wonder that you can remember nothing."

"Someone shot me!" Stephen said flatly. "Melissa says it was Mr Hawkesworth, but I do not believe it. She says it was he who tried to get into my room, too, and dropped that dagger. Or if it was not Mr Hawkesworth, she says, it was Mahdu!"

"It was neither," Perdita told him firmly. "Both Mr Hawkesworth and his servant have proved that they were nowhere near Tarrington Chase that night."

"I never believed it was. Why should they want to do such a thing?" He paused, a frown wrinkling his brow. "Why should anyone wish to, ma'am?"

"I should not vex your mind over that," Perdita said reassuringly. "But there is one thing I would like you to tell me. What made you go to Bryn Morgan's cottage that morning?"

The colour ran up under Stephen's fair skin, and he looked rather shamefaced. "I ought not to have done so, should I, when I had promised you I would not? But I was not going to the cottage, precisely. Bryn was going to take me across to Mays Court, so that Mr Hawkesworth could show me his Indian treasures."

"I do not understand," she said with a frown. "Did he tell you he would do so?"

"It was in the note," Stephen explained. "Two days before, when I went to let Russet out in the morning, there was a note addressed to me pinned to the wall of his kennel. It said that if I went down to the river at that time, Bryn would take me to Mays Court." He looked candidly at her. "Miss Frayne, I know it was very wrong of me to break my promise, and it is only right that you should punish me."

Perdita patted his hand. "I think, my dear, that you have been punished enough," she said dryly. "Did Morgan write the note?"

"Oh, no! Bryn cannot read or write. It was not signed, but I thought it must be from Mr Hawkesworth, and that Bryn had put it there for me to find."

"What has become of it?"

"I threw it into the fire. I didn't want anyone to see it."

Perdita nodded. It probably did not matter, for even if the note were still in existence, it was unlikely to have offered any clue to the identity of its writer. Yet who in the world, apart from Stephen and herself, knew that the boy had had any contact with Jason, and might accept what seemed to be an invitation from him?

"Stephen," she said quietly, "did you tell anyone about meeting Mr Hawkesworth and Mahdu at the cottage?"

"No, ma'am," he replied. "At least, I told Edward that I had seen them there, but he does not know that you were there too. I knew I must say nothing about that."

Edward! For a few moments Perdita's shocked mind grappled with the possibility, but then reluctantly dismissed it. Edward had nothing to gain, and everything to lose. Stephen was the reason for his presence at Tarrington Chase, and if the boy died, Edward would be obliged to earn his living in some far less congenial way.

So although the question of how Stephen had been lured into the trap was now answered, the solution to the mystery was as far to seek, and the danger as great, as ever. Everyone at the Chase was conscious of it, and everyone in Tarrington, too. Gwenny, after her next visit home, had a really sensational piece of news to relate, which made it clear that feelings in the village, far from subsiding, were growing steadily more turbulent.

The previous afternoon, according to Gwenny, Jason had been driving with Miss Delamere in his curricle when at Tarrington Bridge they were surrounded by an angry crowd of men and boys, who hurled abuse, and more tangible tokens of their hostility, impartially at both occupants of the carriage. Jason's hat had been knocked from his head, his clothes, and those of his companion, spattered with filth, and they were only saved from more serious injury by Jason driving his maddened horses straight at the mob, which had to scatter wildly in order to escape the plunging hooves.

Perdita listened with horror to Gwenny's gleeful account of the incident, and was not surprised to hear, some twenty-four hours later, that Miss Delamere and her abigail had left Mays Court in Jason's chaise, bound, so it was rumoured, for London. Clearly, he was sending Alicia out of harm's way; for his own sake, Perdita wished that he had accompanied her.

A few days after this, Lady Tarrington sent for Perdita and told her that at the beginning of the following week she intended to take both children to stay for an indefinite period with their mother's parents at Cheltenham Spa.

"I shall know no peace of mind, Miss Frayne, as long as Jason Hawkesworth is within reach of my grandson," she went on. "Say nothing of this to anyone, and caution Gwenny to keep silent also. I want no one to know—especially not Dr Meredith! He is too closely associated with Hawkesworth."

Perdita went back to the schoolroom wing with a heavy heart. This was probably the best thing that could happen, since with Stephen and Jason some forty miles apart, the latter could not be made the scapegoat for any further attempt against the boy, but it made it even less likely that she and Jason would ever meet again. She would be denied even the small comfort of knowing that he was within reach if danger did threaten.

She decided, as much for her own sake as for Stephen's, that Jason must be told of their imminent departure. She hoped to find an opportunity to send him a message by Owen Meredith, but the doctor was no longer coming regularly to see Stephen, and at last, with only two days left before their departure, desperation made Perdita reckless. Melissa was having her music lesson—the master came from the nearest town twice a week—and Stephen was with Edward. Perdita slipped quietly out of the house down the spiral stair, and set off to walk to the village.

The cold November day was dull and cheerless, and her spirits felt as grey as the weather, shadowed by foreboding about the future. Though nothing more had been said, she felt certain that Lady Tarrington did not mean to keep her on once the three months had passed.

Owen Meredith lived in a square, stone house by the

bridge, and Perdita was fortunate enough to find him at home. When he had heard what she had to tell, he said with approval:

"A wise decision on her ladyship's part! It should be enough to ensure Stephen's safety—though not for the reason she supposes. I would feel happier, though, had it been possible to discover the identity of his enemy."

"Do you suppose, sir," Perdita suggested diffidently, "that Mr Eastly repeated to someone what Stephen told him?"

"As to that," Owen replied bluntly, "I would suspect Eastly himself if I could see any motive he might have, but he could look for no profit in young Stephen's death. The bulk of the Tarrington fortune has to remain in the family, and even if both those children died, there is another branch in Shropshire which would inherit."

"I fear we shall never find out who was responsible," she agreed with a sigh, "but as long as no more attempts are made on Stephen's life, we must be satisfied. Now I must go! It will take me longer to climb the hill than it did to walk down it."

"I shall be driving up there myself in a little while, to the Home Farm," Owen remarked, "and will be glad to take you with me. I have a call to make first at the other end of the village, but if you care to wait here for me, it will save you a long walk, and you will reach the Chase just as quickly."

Perdita accepted gratefully and he went off, first apologising for the fact that since his housekeeper was out, he could offer her no refreshment. Perdita did not want any, but she was glad to sit by the fire in Dr Meredith's shabby, comfortable parlour with its long, low window looking out on to the steeply sloping, walled garden at the back of the house. Until that moment, she had not realised how tired she was from her unceasing vigilance on Stephen's behalf. It was a relief to be alone and quiet in this cheerful room, which was so different from the gloomy grandeur of Tarrington Chase; her tense nerves began to relax for the first time in many troubled weeks. She took off her bonnet and leaned her head thankfully against the high back of her chair. Presently, lulled by the warmth of the fire and the unaccustomed peacefulness of her surroundings, she fell asleep.

She was roused by the sound of the door opening, and sat guiltily upright, embarrassed that Dr Meredith should find her sleeping. He had not. It was Jason who was regarding her from the doorway.

"Have you come to see Dr Meredith?" she stammered. "He will be back directly."

"I have come to see you. Owen sent word that you were here." He closed the door and came across to the fire, looking quizzically down at her. "What is this about going to Cheltenham?"

She told him, glad of the opportunity this gave her to collect the wits scattered by his unexpected arrival. His reaction to the news was similar to Owen's, but he was even more sceptical of the idea of Edward being Stephen's mysterious enemy. Had the purpose of the plot, he said contemptuously, been to keep the boy permanently at home with a tutor, he would have believed it, but he could not imagine Eastly doing anything which would cut short his stay at Tarrington Chase.

"You really believe, then, that in Cheltenham Stephen will be safe?" Perdita asked anxiously. "Oh, how thankful I shall be if that is so!"

"I suppose you have been watching over that confounded child day and night, which is why I found you asleep just now!" Jason remarked. "Yes, I do believe it! Whoever is responsible is determined to cast the blame on my shoulders, and he cannot hope to do that if I am forty miles away."

"But sooner or later Stephen will return to Tarrington," she replied in a troubled voice, "and the bitterness towards you which exists in the village may not have subsided. Her ladyship, I am sure, encourages it, and will continue to do so. You have sent Miss Delamere away for her own safety. Will you not now consider yours?"

There was a pause which to Perdita seemed to drag on for ever, while she wondered apprehensively whether she had been too bold. Then he said reflectively:

"It is true that nothing would have persuaded Alicia to risk a repetition of that incident at the bridge, but even before that I had decided to bring our association to an end." Meeting Perdita's startled glance, he added dryly: "We parted quite amicably, I assure you! She has returned, very thankfully, to London, with the means to live in her accustomed style until she finds a new protector."

Perdita felt an illogical leap of delight. Illogical because it could make no difference to her that Jason had tired of his current mistress, since, if the gossip she had heard were true, he would soon find someone to take

Alicia's place. Yet, even knowing this, she felt as though a weight had been lifted from her heart. Trying to ignore the foolish feeling, she said doubtfully:

"Was it wise, sir, to send Miss Delamere away? It may increase the suspicion against you that you and she should part so soon after she provided you with an alibi."

"It should not, for if I had persuaded her to lie on that occasion she would have had such a hold over me that I would never have dared to be rid of her. But you should know by now that whatever I do increases the suspicion against me! For example, it is now being freely said that when I brought you and Stephen from the river, I was in fact concerned only to rescue the pretty governess!" He paused, observing with an amused eye Perdita's look of confusion, and then added calmly: "For once, rumour happens to be true."

"I wish you would be serious!" she said crossly. "You know that you stand in considerable danger from the hostility against you, and I entreat you to listen to reason! Leave Tarrington! It is the only prudent course!"

He continued to look down at her, one hand resting on the mantelpiece, the other thrust deep into his pocket. She knew a moment's fear that he was angry, and then the firelight, flickering across the dark, piratical face, showed her that he was smiling.

"Very well," he said unexpectedly, "I *will* leave Tarrington—on one condition! That you come with me."

XI

Perdita stared wordlessly at him. She must have misunderstood—yet she knew that she had not. "Come with me," he had said, as though it were the most natural thing in the world. Alicia had gone; had she then been chosen to take Alicia's place? Gladness that he wanted her was strangely overlaid with shock and anger, but the thing which shocked her most of all was that she, the prim governess, the sheltered daughter of the Vicarage, wanted more than anything to answer simply, "I will come."

"I do not think, sir," she said faintly at last, striving desperately for dignity, "that a jest of that nature is amusing."

"I was not jesting!" He bent suddenly and grasped

her hands, pulling her to her feet. "Marry me, Perdita!"

"Marry you?" This was even more unbelievable.
"You are asking me to be—your wife?"

The black brows lifted. "Why the devil should you
suppose I meant anything else?"

"Why . . . ?" She gave a little gasp of laughter. "Oh,
why should I not? Men in your position do not usually
propose *marriage* to a woman in mine."

"It is what *I* am proposing," he assured her, but then
his expression changed and hardened. "But when a
man asks a woman to be his wife, he should have a
name to offer her! One which is his by right! I should
have remembered that."

She sensed the pain behind the sudden coldness of
his voice, and, pulling one hand free, laid her fingers
fleetingly on his lips to check the bitter words.

"Do you think *that* matters to me?" she said softly.
"It does not! It never could! But I never supposed
. . . ! It seemed so unlikely that you would ever marry."

"I never wanted to," he replied frankly, "until I met
you. I shall probably be a damnable husband, but if
you will have me, my dear, I'll do my best to make you
happy."

She looked shyly up at him, and read in the tawny
eyes all that the careless words left unsaid. Happiness
flooded over her, and her hand tightened in his clasp,
returning the pressure of his.

"I have often thought," she murmured, "that a *perfect* husband would be rather trying."

He laughed, and swept her into a crushing embrace
to which she responded in a manner wholly unbecom-
ing in a staid governess. She had forgotten, in fact, that

she was a governess; that she had slipped away from her duties without leave from her employer; and that she ought at that moment to be in the schoolroom at Tarrington Chase instead of in Dr Meredith's parlour, being very thoroughly kissed by the man whose mere name was hated in her employer's house. It was the tall clock in the corner, wheezily chiming the hour, which eventually recalled these facts to her mind. She gave a gasp of dismay.

"Oh, I must go! Melissa's music lesson will be over, and I meant to be there when she comes back to the schoolroom!"

Jason frowned. "There is no need for you to go back," he said abruptly. "Never again!"

"But I cannot simply walk out without saying a word, and not return," she protested, laughing. "Besides, everything I possess is at Tarrington Chase. My clothes, all my personal belongings . . . ! I must go back."

"I will buy you everything you need. As for sending word, it will give me great pleasure to write to Lady Tarrington, informing her that you have done me the honour of accepting my proposal of marriage, and will therefore not be returning to her house." He grinned. "I'll wager your property will be packed up and sent after you in a very short space of time!"

"Very likely!" Perdita tried to speak severely, but there was a betraying quiver of laughter in her voice. "And where, pray, am I to go if I do not return to Tarrington Chase? It would not be proper for me to stay at Mays Court."

"Devil take propriety!" He was looking at her in a way which made her heart beat faster and deepened the colour in her cheeks. "It might not be prudent, though! You can spend the night here, with Owen's housekeeper for chaperon. Tomorrow we'll drive up to London. You shall stay at the most respectable hotel I can find, and first thing the next morning I will obtain a special licence, and we can be married."

For a few dazzled, delightful moments Perdita allowed herself to consider the suggestion. It sounded so simple, and she had no doubt that Jason would make it so; he was the kind of man for whom obstacles existed only to be swept aside. She loved him so much, and in two days' time she could be his wife. She need never go back to Tarrington Chase, to the gloomy, panelled rooms of the schoolroom wing, or the formal grandeur of the drawing-room where Lady Tarrington sat implacably enthroned beneath the portrait of her dead son.

She was about to agree when there flashed into her mind the memory of Stephen's pale, thin little face, with its golden eyes so like the beloved ones now looking into hers. The child was fond of her, and he lived still in the grim shadow of attempted murder. It would be heartless to desert him.

"I cannot," she said in a low voice. "I must go back, for Stephen's sake. Oh, Jason, try to understand! I am sure that as long as he is here, he is in danger! Let me stay with him until he is safe at his grandfather's house in Cheltenham. It will be for only a few days, and I would never forgive myself if some harm befell him that I might have prevented had I been there."

Jason hesitated. He shared Perdita's belief in Stephen's danger, and he was convinced that during the next day or two it would be more pressing than ever

before, for if the boy's enemy knew he was going away
—and he seemed uncannily well informed—he would
realise that time was running out. If Jason himself, already under suspicion for the previous vain attempts,
were to be blamed for a successful one, the blow would
have to be struck while he and Stephen were still in
Tarrington.

Yet if Stephen were in danger, so also was Perdita.
Twice she had saved the child's life, and her constant
watchfulness must make her the biggest stumbling
block in the would-be murderer's path; it was only
logical to suppose that he would try to remove her.
Jason wished Stephen no harm, but, with the single-
mindedness of a man deeply and whole-heartedly in
love for the first time in his life, he was concerned only
to protect Perdita.

The very fact that she meant so much to him, however, made it difficult for him to deny her. She would
probably do as he wished, but she would fret and worry
over Stephen if she did not go back now to Tarrington
Chase. So with the utmost reluctance, which subsequent events were to prove well justified, he said
slowly:

"I understand, but I do not like it, for if there *is*
danger I want you safely out of it. But I suppose I must
let you have your own way! When do you leave for
Cheltenham?"

"On the day after tomorrow."

He nodded. "Very well! On the day after that I shall
come for you!"

"Not to Cheltenham!" Perdita's voice was sharp
with alarm. "Jason, you must not follow us there! Oh,
promise me that you will not!"

He realised that she was right, and that to do so might be to play into the criminal's hands.

"My carriage will come for you, then," he said. "I will take the curricle, and wait for you at Oxford. Then we can go on together to London." He took her by the shoulders, looking down at her with a smile which yet had seriousness behind it. "If you fail me, I shall come to Cheltenham and carry you off. I do not intend you to escape from me!"

"Do you think I want to?" she replied softly. "I did not know it was possible to be as happy as I am at this moment."

That happiness stayed with her, warm and reassuring, even when she had parted from him to return to Tarrington Chase. Owen Meredith set her down at the tall gates with their guardian griffons, and she hurried along the winding drive, through a raw November dusk which seemed to her as beautiful as high summer.

A shock awaited her when she reached the entrance to the spiral stair, for during her absence the door had been bolted on the inside. She hesitated for a few moments, and then hastened breathlessly round to the door the servants used, and went through the stone-flagged passages of the kitchen regions hoping against hope that she might still reach the schoolroom wing unobserved.

This was not to be. She had to pass the housekeeper's room, and Mrs Price was evidently watching for her. She came out as Perdita was walking quietly past, and said sharply:

"Her ladyship be waiting to see you, miss! Said you was to be sent to her the instant you come in. Very angry with you she is!"

Perdita's heart sank, for this meant that there was going to be an unpleasant scene. She went reluctantly to answer that peremptory summons, and one glance at the old lady's face was enough to tell her that Lady Tarrington was more angry than ever before. Not with the insensate fury which only Jason seemed to provoke in her, but with the cold anger of a domestic tyrant whose wishes had been disregarded. She sat by her sitting-room fire, erect and implacable, the downward curve of her lips even more pronounced than usual, her pale eyes hard and cold as ice. Edward, in riding-dress, was standing by the window.

"Where have you been, Miss Frayne?" Lady Tarrington demanded as soon as Perdita was inside the room. "I did not give you permission to leave the house."

"I am sorry, my lady!" Perdita spoke meekly, although she resented the tone, and resented even more that she should be spoken to in that fashion in front of Edward. "I went to the village."

"For what purpose?"

"To see Dr Meredith." It was useless to pretend otherwise. "I thought there could be no objection. Miss Tarrington was at her music lesson, and Sir Stephen studying with Mr Eastly."

"It is not for you to decide when your presence is or is not required. Mr Eastly found it necessary to go out. He sent Stephen back to the schoolroom, assuming, of course, that you would be there. As a result, Stephen wandered about the gardens for an hour and more, entirely alone, a thing which, with good reason, I have expressly forbidden. Why did you go to see Dr Meredith?"

The question, coming so suddenly in the midst of a rebuke, took Perdita unawares. She stared at Lady Tarrington, not knowing how to reply.

"Are you unwell, Miss Frayne? If you are, Dr Meredith could have been sent for. It is my custom to look after the health of everyone in my service."

"I am perfectly well, ma'am, thank you."

"Then why did you visit the doctor?"

"It was a private matter," Perdita said desperately.

"A private matter!" Lady Tarrington repeated the words with the utmost contempt. Her cold gaze raked Perdita from head to foot. "When a young, unmarried woman goes furtively to consult a physician on a matter of such extreme privacy, there is usually only one inference to be drawn!" She lifted her hand to check the indignant protest which Perdita, her cheeks flaming scarlet, had started to make. "I am not concerned to know whether or not that inference is correct. You are dismissed, Miss Frayne! I find you impertinent, untrustworthy, and of a character totally unfitted to be entrusted with the care of the young."

From scarlet, Perdita's face became white, though this was caused by anger and not, as both Lady Tarrington and Edward supposed, by dismay. She said in a low voice:

"I will go and pack. Does your ladyship wish me to leave Tarrington Chase tonight?"

"No, Miss Frayne, I do not! It does not suit my convenience to be left with no one to complete the children's preparations for their visit to Cheltenham. You will attend to that, and make the journey with us, and then you will leave. I shall find it easier to fill the situation there."

For a moment Perdita toyed with the idea of retorting that it did not suit her convenience to remain any longer at Tarrington Chase; that she would leave immediately, and seek the protection of her future husband. Then prudence overcame temptation. For Stephen's sake she could endure two more days of humiliation, in order to leave him safe in Cheltenham, her conscience clear.

She said nothing to the children of her imminent departure, being as reluctant to upset Stephen as she was to give his sister cause for rejoicing. Later that evening, when the little boy had gone to bed, and Melissa was in her own room, she began to gather together the books and other things belonging to her which, during the past three months, had found their way into the schoolroom.

She was interrupted by Edward, who strolled in, immaculate in the evening dress he always wore to dine with Lady Tarrington, and leaned idly against the table to watch her. They had not spoken since the uncomfortable scene in her ladyship's sitting-room.

"It seems that our acquaintance is to be cut short, Miss Frayne," he remarked at length. "I cannot tell you how sorry I am!"

"You are very kind!" Perdita spoke distantly, for the suspicion that he was mocking her had crossed her mind. "It is exceedingly unfortunate, however, that you did not inform me that Stephen would not, after all, be in your charge all the afternoon."

"I did not know, ma'am! Something occurred, quite unexpectedly, which made it necessary for me to leave him."

She bit back an angry retort. Edward, of course, could come and go as he pleased, even abandoning his pupil in the middle of a lesson, without earning any rebuke from Lady Tarrington. It was nothing to him that Perdita had been dismissed because of it; that she was, for all he knew, to be abandoned in a strange town with very little money and practically no hope of obtaining another situation. It occurred to her, not for the first time, that in spite of his charming manners, Edward Eastly was one of the most selfish people she had ever met.

"No purpose can be served by talking of it," she said at last. "I did something of which I knew Lady Tarrington would disapprove, and I was found out. I guessed what the consequences of *that* would be!"

"Perhaps it need not be!" Edward moved round the table until he was close beside her where she stood putting her books into a neat pile. "I have some influence with her ladyship! Perhaps I can persuade her to give you another chance."

Perdita uttered a little, scornful laugh. "I fear you flatter your powers of persuasion, Mr Eastly! You cannot seriously suppose that Lady Tarrington would relent, after the things she said to me this afternoon?"

"She was angry then, and disturbed about Stephen, but by tomorrow she will be in a calmer mood and I can probably prevail upon her to listen to reason. You would be grateful, would you not, if I could do so?"

"I am grateful, sir, that you should think of it, but I do not believe—"

"How grateful?" he interrupted, laying his hand on hers. "How grateful would you be, Miss Frayne?"

For a second or two surprise held her motionless, and even anger was in abeyance. Then she said indignantly:

"I do not understand you, Mr Eastly! Or rather, I prefer not to understand! I think we should both forget that remark was ever made!"

She tried to pull her hand away as she spoke, but his grip on it tightened painfully, and when she turned to him in angry protest he reached out and grasped the other hand also, holding her prisoner. He was standing close against her, so that, trapped by the heavy table behind her, she could not escape; and at that inopportune moment, Melissa walked into the room.

She stopped short in the doorway, staring incredulously, her lips parted and her eyes wide with shocked disbelief. Then with an incoherent exclamation she turned and fled.

Edward swore softly. His grip relaxed, and Perdita was able to pull herself free and whisk away to the other side of the table. From that point of comparative safety—she was now closer to the door than he was—she said in a voice trembling with anger:

"I think you must have taken leave of your senses! What have I ever done to make you suppose you could treat me in so ungentlemanly a fashion? I have a very good mind to complain to Lady Tarrington!"

"Do so, if you think she will believe you!" Edward retorted. His face was flushed, and there was a sneering look about his mouth. "I warn you that my version of the incident will be totally different, and I fancy that *my* credit in that quarter is better than yours. Besides, are you not being very improvident? I may be able to save you from dismissal, and will endeavour to do so if I can be sure you will be properly grateful, while if you *are* turned off in Cheltenham without a reference—for she will not give you one, you know—you will be in still more urgent need of a friend. A protector!"

Perdita looked at him. Her glance swept over him from head to foot and then lifted again to his face, and the contempt in her eyes made his cheeks darken still further. "And if I do," she said in a tone which matched the look, "I would sooner it were any man in the world than you! You may think you have forced me into an impossible situation—I believe you knew I had gone out this afternoon, and left Stephen alone deliberately—but you can be sure that nothing on earth could persuade me to accept help from *you!*"

Without giving him a chance to reply she went quickly out of the schoolroom and into her bedchamber next to it. Closing the door, she stood leaning against it and trying to recover her composure, for Edward's sudden amorous advances had come as a severe shock, and she felt shamed as well as angry.

She had forgotten Melissa's part in the incident, but she was soon to be reminded of it in no uncertain fashion. The door flew open, with no preliminary knock, and the girl burst into the room. Her hair was untidy and her eyes red from weeping, but the look in her face was extraordinarily reminiscent of her grandmother. She slammed the door and leaned against it, as Perdita had leaned earlier, staring at her governess across the width of the room.

"I know what you are trying to do, Miss Frayne!"

she announced. "You are trying to trap Edward into marrying you, but he will not! I know that he will not!"

"I am trying to do nothing of the kind, Miss Tarrington, and that is an exceedingly foolish way to talk," Perdita replied with as much dignity as she could. "These are matters of which you know nothing, that you are too young to understand."

"I do understand!" Melissa's voice was trembling now. She was finding it impossible to maintain her pose of cold composure. "I saw you with him in the schoolroom just now, and you have been flirting shamelessly with him ever since you came here, but you shall not have him! You shall not! Edward won't marry a little nobody of a governess! He is going to marry me!"

"You are a very silly little girl," Perdita said angrily, "and it is most improper for you to talk in this way. Go back to your room, and go to bed."

"I won't go to bed! I am going straight to tell Grandmama what I saw just now, and then she will dismiss you!" Melissa was sobbing again. "I want you to be dismissed! I hate you!"

"I shall be leaving you in any event as soon as we reach Cheltenham," Perdita said coldly, "so there is no need for you to carry tales to her ladyship." She paused, studying Melissa's tear-streaked face. She disliked the girl, and she was angry with her, but she was young enough herself to remember how real and agonising a romantic infatuation could be when one was fourteen. "Pray do not cry, Miss Tarrington! Mr Eastly's behaviour this evening must have shown you how unworthy of your regard he is, and it is far too soon for you to be talking, or even thinking about marriage. In four or five years' time, when you have entered Society, and some eligible gentleman seeks your grandmama's permission to address you, you will recall this evening, and smile over it."

"I will not! Edward is not to blame for what happened tonight! It was all your fault! And it *is* true that he will marry me when I am grown-up! Grandmama said so!"

Something in Melissa's tone carried conviction. Perdita, staring at her, said slowly: "Even if her ladyship were considering such an arrangement, she would hardly discuss it with you at this stage."

Melissa flushed, and said with considerably less assurance: "She did not discuss it with me. She and Edward were talking about it last summer, when they did not know that I was anywhere near. I . . . I just happened to hear what they said."

In plain words, Perdita thought grimly, you were eavesdropping; and the admission convinced her, as nothing else could have done, that Melissa was speaking the truth. She found that she was trembling, for the implications of the discovery were staggering. With a tremendous effort she steadied her voice sufficiently to say:

"If that is so, Miss Tarrington, you should have disregarded it. Certainly you should not have repeated it to anyone. Her ladyship would be very angry, and rightly so, if she knew. Now please go back to your room, and let us forget that this most unseemly conversation ever took place."

For a moment she thought that Melissa was going to defy her, but much of her belligerence seemed to have deserted her. Perhaps she was regretting her disclosure, and frightened of what would happen if her grandmother learned of it, for after only a brief hesitation she went off meekly enough.

Perdita sank down on the edge of the bed. So Edward was to marry Melissa, and whether the notion were Lady Tarrington's own, or whether Edward himself had managed to put it into her head, was not important. What was important was the fact that Melissa would inherit the entire estate if her brother died.

Was it possible for Edward to have made the three attempts on Stephen's life? He had been away from Tarrington at the time of the second, but there was only his word that he had gone straight home to Staffordshire, while the note enticing Stephen into the trap had been placed in Russet's kennel before his departure. The other two murder attempts could easily have been his doing.

The longer Perdita thought about it, the more convinced of his guilt she became, and with conviction came deepening fear. She saw now what Jason had perceived earlier—that this was Stephen's time of greatest danger. For the next thirty-six hours or so he would be in mortal peril from the man in whose charge he spent much of his time, and whom his grandmother trusted beyond anyone else.

Panic swept over her. The responsibility was so great to bear alone, yet bear it she must until the following day, for there was no hope of summoning Jason to her aid that night. The clouds which had hung low and thick all day were now obscuring the moon, and in that dense darkness she dare not attempt the steep woodland path to Bryn Morgan's cottage, while by this time the lodge gates would be locked, barring the road to the village. Tomorrow she must find some way of sending a message, but for the present Stephen's safety, and therefore Jason's safety, too, rested in her hands alone.

XII

The problem of sending the message, which Perdita
had brooded over at intervals throughout a sleepless
night, was solved for her in an unexpected way. When
she went into the schoolroom before breakfast, an agitated Gwenny told her that her mother had been taken
ill, and that Lady Tarrington had given her leave to go
home for a few days, to nurse the invalid and look after
the younger members of the family. One of the other
maids would be taking over her duties in the schoolroom wing until her return.

To Perdita, this was a heaven-sent opportunity, and
Gwenny, when asked to deliver a note to Dr Meredith's
house on her way home, agreed without hesitation.
Perdita scribbled a hasty note to Jason, telling him

what she had found out and asking him to meet her at
the end of the Long Walk at ten o'clock that night; she
folded the paper inside another sheet addressed to
Owen, sealed it, and gave it to Gwenny with an earnest
entreaty to her not to forget it. She wished she could
have asked Jason to come earlier, but did not want him
to risk approaching Tarrington Chase in daylight, when
any of the outdoor servants might see him, and when
she would have little hope of slipping out alone.

She hated to see Stephen leave her to join Edward in
the library, even though common sense told her that he
was unlikely to be in any immediate danger. Common
sense brought very little comfort to Perdita that day.
She was overwrought and very tired, for she had spent
the night lying half dressed on her bed, with the door of
her room propped open far enough to enable her to see
Stephen's door on the other side of the corridor. The
slightest sound had been sufficient to jerk her awake,
and such sleep as she had had was haunted by evil
dreams.

Both Stephen and Melissa were excited at the prospect of an indefinite stay in Cheltenham, and from remarks they had let fall Perdita formed the impression
that their maternal grandparents were very different
from Lady Tarrington. There were numerous other
grandchildren besides themselves, and some of these
frequently shared a visit with the young Tarringtons.
Perdita hoped that some of them had been invited on
this occasion; the company of other children would do
much to lift the shadow of recent grim events at Tarrington Chase.

When lessons were over for the day, she took her

charges for a short walk, since the skies were clearing now and it was bright, though cold. Afterwards they went to say goodbye to Nurse, a ceremony which always had to be carried out if they were going away. Perdita, looking at the old woman as the children talked to her, thought that this might well be the last time they would do so. Nurse had failed alarmingly in the three months since Perdita's first meeting with her. She was more wizened and doll-like than ever, and the sharpness had left her tongue just as the shrewd brightness was fading from her eyes. Probably, Perdita reflected, the danger which threatened Stephen, and of which Nurse, of course, was aware, was largely to blame. It was plain that she adored the little boy. She kept him beside her throughout the visit, holding his hand in her withered fingers, and scarcely taking her eyes from his face.

Just as they were leaving, she called Perdita back, and beckoned to her to bend close. "I do hear tell you be leaving for good," she muttered. "Be it so?"

"Yes, it is," Perdita replied in a low voice. "Lady Tarrington has dismissed me."

"Then us must talk tonight! There be summat as I do want to tell, look, and you'm the only one I can trust. The only one who ain't beholden to my lady for one thing or t'other. You come back, mind! Later on, when the babbies be in bed."

Perdita nodded. She could not imagine what Nurse wanted to tell her, but there was something in the faded eyes—the look, it seemed, of a trapped creature desperately seeking a way of escape—which sent a little prickle of apprehension through her. The old woman

was grievously troubled, and even in the midst of her
own fears, Perdita had not the heart to refuse her.

"I will come," she said gently, "as soon as I can. I
give you my word."

Nurse nodded thankfully, and relaxed again upon
her pillows, and Perdita followed the children from the
room. When she looked back from the doorway, the
old servant's eyes were closed and her lips moving
soundlessly. She looked as though she might be praying.

The visit to the drawing-room was cut short that
evening, Lady Tarrington telling the children that they
must go early to bed because of the journey on the
morrow. Perdita was relieved, for she was anxious to
keep her promise to Nurse, and had been afraid that
she might not have time to do so before going to meet
Jason.

Stephen was disconsolate at the news, triumphantly
imparted to him by Melissa, that Perdita was leaving.
He had made her promise that she would go to his
room to bid him good night, and when Bessie, the maid
who was taking Gwenny's place, came to the schoolroom with the usual glass of hot milk for Melissa—
Stephen had his in bed—she went to do so. As she
stepped out into the corridor she heard a faint sound,
and looked quickly round in time to see the great oak
door which gave access to the main part of the house
being softly closed.

She stared at it, and then with a sudden surge of
alarm ran towards Stephen's room, for Bessie was still
tending the schoolroom fire, and the door could not
have closed by itself. To her relief all seemed to be
well. Stephen was sitting up in bed playing with Russet,

who, in defiance of all orders, was sprawled across his lap, and he shook his head in surprise when Perdita asked him if anyone had come in.

"Only Bessie, with my milk," he replied. "Why, Miss Frayne?"

"I thought perhaps Mr Eastly had been to say good night!" Perdita spoke as lightly as she could. "I thought I saw him leaving the corridor as I came from the schoolroom."

"Why should Edward come to say good night, ma'am? He never does so!"

"If he did not, it does not matter," Perdita said firmly. "I must have been mistaken. Russet, you bad dog, get down from the bed this instant! You know, Sir Stephen, your grandmama would not allow you to keep Russet with you at night if she knew how you let him behave."

"She would, because he is here to guard me," Stephen informed her, but he pushed the dog from the bed and ordered him sternly to his mat in the corner. Russet went reluctantly. "Oh, Miss Frayne, I wish you were not going away! Why can you not stay with us in Cheltenham?"

"Your grandmama does not wish me to, my dear, and I have to do as she says. You will soon learn to like your new governess." She paused, looking down at the disconsolate little face and golden-brown eyes, and then bent and kissed his cheek. "I shall miss you, Stephen!"

He had all a ten-year-old boy's contempt for sentimentality, but he flung his arms round her neck and gave her a bear-like hug. Perdita held him close for a moment, and then straightened up and said briskly, trying to ignore her suddenly smarting eyes:

"Come now, drink your milk and then go to sleep, for we have a long journey to make tomorrow. Bessie will be in directly to fetch your glass and put out the light."

She handed him the glass of milk, which he accepted with a grimace, and watched him begin to sip it. Then she went back to the schoolroom, where she waited with concealed impatience until Melissa, too, had gone to bed, leaving her free to hurry to Nurse's room.

The old woman was watching for her, and as soon as Perdita came to her bedside, reached out to clutch her hand, saying in an urgent whisper:

"Do anyone know you'm here?"

"No, no one," Perdita replied soothingly, studying the white, wizened face as well as she could by the light of the single candle. "Nurse, what is troubling you so?"

"Troubling me? Aye!" Nurse said bitterly. "I be an old woman, my dearie, wi' not long to live, look, and there be a grievous weight o' wickedness on my soul. Evil do breed evil, and the sins o' long ago begets them as do plague us now! The little lad be under the shadow o' death, but my lady won't lift it from 'un, look, just by taking 'un away! Him'll follow, or else bide patient till they do come back to Tarrington. Him don't forgive nor forget. Never did, mind, even when 'un was a lad."

"Are you speaking now of Jason Hawkesworth?" Perdita asked doubtfully, for she had had difficulty in following the rambling words. "Nurse, it is not he who threatens Stephen. I swear it is not!"

"O' course it be him!" Nurse said scornfully. "But it ain't the little lad he do hate, look! It be my lady, for what her done to his mam. Aye, and to him, too, though him don't know that. But I do know, mind, and I do know as I've kept silent too long. 'Twas for the little lad's sake I said naught, and anyway, us all thought young Jason were dead. So many years, and no word of 'un! But now him have come back, and it be time the truth was told. 'Twill give 'un the revenge 'un wants on my lady, and the little lad'll be safe at last!"

"What is the truth, Nurse?" Perdita spoke as patiently as she could, for she was beginning to think that the old woman's mind was wandering. "If you want me to help you, you will have to tell me."

"That be why I told you to come," Nurse retorted with a flash of her old tartness. "The truth be this, look! Tarrington do belong by rights to young Jason, for his mam were Sir Humphrey's lawful wife."

There was a moment of utter silence, and then Perdita said in a stunned voice: "What did you say?"

"Jason Hawkesworth be Sir Humphrey's lawful son!" Nurse repeated stubbornly. "Sir Humphrey told me so when him lay dying."

Perdita put her hand to her head. "I do not understand! If Susan Hawkesworth were married to Sir Humphrey, how . . . ? Why . . . ?"

Nurse told her. The story rambled a good deal, but Perdita found it easy to be patient now, and slowly she unravelled the incredible tale. Sir Humphrey had married Susan in London soon after they met, but he had not dared to disclose the marriage to anyone, least of all to his uncle, his erstwhile guardian, who was even then arranging for him to marry an heiress. Hopelessly in debt, pestered by creditors and fearful of his uncle's anger, Humphrey—who seemed to have been a charming but weak young man—had found himself caught in a tide of events he lacked the courage to halt, and had gone through a ceremony of "marriage" with the rich bride chosen for him.

In his true wife he was more fortunate than he deserved, for she loved him deeply. Too deeply to ruin him by disclosing the truth when at last he confessed it to her, and too deeply to part from him. She had chosen the only other path open to her, the incredibly hard path of spending the rest of her life as his "mistress", and of seeing another woman in her rightful place. She demanded only one thing in return—that Humphrey should make certain that, when he died, their son would inherit everything which was his by right.

Sir Humphrey had made a Will in Jason's favour, and bestowed it, together with the documents proving his marriage to Susan and the legitimacy of Jason's birth, in a secure hiding-place against the time when they should be needed. Perhaps he would also have told Jason himself the truth when he reached manhood, had the boy remained in Tarrington, but Jason, reckless and arrogant, embittered by the taunts he had endured throughout his life, had gone, and the truth remained a secret known only to Sir Humphrey and his wife.

Death had come suddenly to Humphrey Tarrington, early in his vigorous middle-age. A young horse, a fall at an awkward fence, hours of lying helpless and injured before his servants found him. Dr Meredith had been called away to a remote farm, and the squire's hurts were far beyond the skill of any of his household to deal with. They had done what they could to ease his suffering, but it was plain to all of them that he was dying. Sir Humphrey himself knew it, and in his conscious moments begged repeatedly for Susan to be brought to him.

"Us'd have fetched her willing enough," Nurse concluded, "for it be a grievous thing to deny a dying man. But my lady swore that even if us did, her'd not let Mrs Hawkesworth set foot inside the house. Her meant it, too! Her'd always hated Susan Hawkesworth, because her was so beautiful and Sir Humphrey loved her. There'd never been aught but hate, look, 'twixt him and my lady!"

Perdita shuddered, thinking of three lives terribly and inextricably tangled in love and hate, and enduring that bitter bondage for thirty years. How deeply Susan Tarrington must have loved her husband, and what courage she must have possessed to remain loyal and silent.

"It were coming evening, I mind," Nurse was saying, "and I were watching beside Sir Humphrey in the Great Bedchamber. More nor once I thought him'd gone, look, so still and quiet him lay, but all at once his eyes opened. 'Nurse,' him says in his poor, weak voice, 'you must help me. There be a great wrong to be righted afore I dies.' Then him told me as how him and Susan was man and wife, and their lad the heir o' Tarrington, and him begged me to find the papers as proved it, and take 'em to her. 'Where be they?' I says. 'Tell me where they be hid.' But instead him looks at summat behind me, and such a look in his face as I'd never seen afore, and pray God I'll never see again.

"I looked round, and my lady were standing behind me in the shadows. How long her'd been there I don't know, but long enough to hear the truth. Her stood there for a moment, wi' her face as white as death and her eyes blazing, and then her pushed me out o' the way and bent over the bed. 'Where be they?' her says, fierce-like. 'Where be these lying papers?' Him wouldn't answer, so her took him by the shoulders and shook him, God forgive her—and him dying! 'Where?' her kept saying. 'Where?' But him never spoke, and in the end her lets go. 'Him be dead!' her says, cold as ice, and then her turns to me. 'You'll say naught o' this to anyone,' her says. 'Jason Hawkesworth be gone from Tarrington these ten years, and belike him be dead by now, and I'll not have my grandson dispossessed and myself shamed for that woman's sake. Bide silent, and I'll see you be well cared for till the end o' your days.' "

The faint old voice ceased, and there was silence for a space. Perdita was thinking of Jason, and of what this would mean to him. Yet, since the proof could not be found, might not Nurse's disclosure be more curse than blessing; might it not deepen his bitterness to know that though the stigma he had borne all his life was unjustified, it must still be borne for ever? Should she tell him, or should she keep silent?

"So I said naught," Nurse resumed after a little while. "Not so much for fear o' my lady as because o' the little lad. Her searched for them papers—aye, and made me search, too—but her never found 'em. And her gave poor Susan no peace. Seemed like all her hate were turned on that one poor woman, till in the end her couldn't stand it no more, and her killed herself. Reck-

on her thought there weren't nothing left to live for, wi'
her husband dead, and her son, too, for all her knew."

"But he came back," Perdita said in a low voice,
"and had it not been for Lady Tarrington's vindictiveness might have found his mother alive. Oh, it is no
wonder he is bitter!"

"Evil do beget evil," Nurse said resignedly. "I
begged my lady to tell the truth, look, but her'd die
afore her did that. Her thinks I be too old and feeble to
cross her, but her be wrong. You do know the truth
now, look, and must make it known. You'm the only
one here as won't go running to my lady wi' the tale
I've told."

"No, I will not do that," Perdita agreed dryly, "but
even if I tell this story, it will not be believed without
proof."

"You'm going to have the proof, my dearie! Sir
Humphrey's Will, and the other papers him hid with
it."

Perdita stared. "You said they could not be found!"

"I said my lady never found 'em. I know where they
be!" She gave a feeble cackle of laughter. "All the time
her were searching, I knew. I seen 'em the day after Sir
Humphrey died."

"Where?" Perdita's voice was unsteady with excitement. "Where are they now?"

"Still where Sir Humphrey hid 'em, in the old hidey-
hole in the nursery—what you do call the schoolroom.
Him found it by chance when him wasn't no more nor
six year old, and only him and me knew of it. Hid all
his bits o' treasures there, him did, and I guessed 'twas
there him had put the papers. Listen careful now, while

I tells how to find it. It be behind the middle panel in
the bottom row 'twixt the window and the fireplace.
You'm to press hard on the top left-hand corner o' that
panel, and on the middle o' the one next to it on the
right, at the same time. It do slide open, look, and
there be a bit of a cupboard behind it." She stretched
out a withered claw to grip Perdita's hand; her eyes
glittered in the candlelight. "You'm to fetch them papers from there, mind, and take 'em to young Jason
afore you sets out tomorrow."

"I promise you that I will," Perdita said unsteadily.
"He will be very grateful to you, Nurse!"

"I do want no thanks from him!" The old woman
released her and sank back against her pillows. "Him'll
have it all now! The Chase, the name o' Tarrington,
revenge on my lady for what his mam suffered. There'll
be no call for him to hurt the little lad!"

Perdita could see that it would be useless to try to
convince her of Jason's innocence; she could only be
thankful that belief in his guilt had prompted Nurse to
reveal what she knew. She repeated her promise to take
the proof to him—Nurse could not know with how
glad a heart she would perform that errand—and hastened eagerly back to the schoolroom.

As she went through the house, a glance at a clock
showed her that there was an hour and more to wait
before she went to meet Jason. To search for the papers would take only a little while, and she wondered
how she was to find the patience to pass the remaining
time. She went through into the schoolroom wing and
closed the massive door quietly, for she did not want to
risk waking either of the children. She hastened eagerly
into the schoolroom and then stopped short, with diffi-

culty suppressing a cry. Edward was sitting beside the fire.

He got up as she entered. "Did I startle you, Miss Frayne?"

She tried to hide the alarm his presence had provoked. Her instinctive reaction was an urgent desire to assure herself at once of Stephen's safety, but she knew that to give way to it would be to risk betraying her knowledge of Edward's intentions towards the child. Surely if he had harmed the boy in any way he would not be waiting calmly for her to return?

"I did not expect to find you here," she said coldly. "What do you want?"

"That is not a very friendly greeting!"

She was suddenly afraid that he meant to renew the importunities of the previous evening, and became instantly and uncomfortably aware of the isolation of that part of the house. Remaining prudently close to the door, she said in the same distant tone:

"I am endeavouring to be civil, Mr Eastly, but that is as much as you can expect. Now, if you will excuse me, I must see that the children are asleep, and after that I have packing to finish, so I will bid you good night."

She went out, deciding that after she had looked in on Stephen and Melissa she would retreat to her own room, in the hope that Edward would go away, but she wondered rather uneasily what she would do if he did not. She took up the lamp from the corridor shelf and opened Melissa's door, shielding the light with her hand. The bed remained in shadow, but the girl's deep, even breathing indicated that she was asleep.

In Stephen's room, Russet lifted his head as the door opened, but Perdita spoke to him in a whisper and he subsided again. Stephen, too, was sleeping, curled up with one hand under his cheek, and she was pierced suddenly with pity and with sorrow as she realised for the first time what disclosure of the truth would mean to him. If it were for anyone other than Jason, she did not think she could have brought herself to tell it.

She went back into the corridor, and as she put down the lamp and took up her own candle to light it, Edward came out of the schoolroom. He stood for a moment watching her, and then said, in a mocking tone which puzzled her and raised a faint stirring of uneasiness:

"Have you satisfied yourself, ma'am, that both your charges are sleeping soundly?"

"Yes," Perdita replied tartly, "I have, and as I do not wish them to be disturbed, we will not stand talking here!"

"Oh, I agree with you, ma'am! This draughty corridor is no place for conversation! Let us go back into the schoolroom."

With a quick movement which took her by surprise, he twisted the candlestick from her grasp, set it down, and, clipping his arm about her waist, swept her with him into the schoolroom before she had a chance to protest. Releasing her, he thrust the door shut and leaned his shoulders against it.

"Have you gone mad?" she demanded with breathless indignation. "Let me out immediately!"

Even as she spoke, she realised that the demand was useless, and turned to reach for the bell-rope, only to pause with outstretched hand, staring in blank bewilderment. The rope no longer hung in its usual place.

Edward chuckled. "Look higher, ma'am!"

13

She did so. The rope had gone, cut neatly through a few inches from the ceiling. She swung round again to Edward.

"You *are* mad! Why go to the trouble of doing that when I have only to call to Stephen, and send him to fetch the servants?"

Edward laughed again, and there was something in the laughter which laid a cold finger of fear on Perdita's heart.

"Call as loudly as you please, my dear Miss Frayne! I assure you that Melissa will sleep soundly until morning in spite of any outcry you may make, while Stephen is in a sleep now from which he will never awaken in this world!"

XIII

Perdita groped behind her for the table and leaned against its solid support. "You are lying!" she said in a shaken whisper. "You must be lying!"

"I assure you I am not! Laudanum, Miss Frayne! I stopped the maid who was bringing the children their hot milk, and distracted her attention with a trivial complaint while I put the drug into it. How fortunate that they each have their own, distinctive glass!" He paused, regarding her with mock solicitude. "I fear this has come as a shock to you, ma'am. Pray sit down! You will recover your composure directly."

She ignored this advice; in fact she scarcely heard it. She did not doubt what Edward had told her, and was remembering with bitter remorse how she had insisted upon Stephen drinking the milk. He did not like it, and always had to be urged to take it. If only she had been lenient on this, her last night in charge of him. If only she had questioned the servant after she saw that mysteriously closing door.

Edward was still complacently watching her, and now a new question and a new fear took shape in her mind.

"Why tell me this?" Try as she would, she could not prevent her voice from trembling. "You know that I will inform against you."

"Of course you would, but as the opportunity will not occur I take no risk. Besides, it seems only just to explain to you, since you are going to be blamed for the murder."

"*I* am to be blamed?"

"You must see, ma'am," he pointed out reasonably, "that if I am not to be suspected, I must provide a culprit. I was obliged to give up the notion of implicating Hawkesworth directly in the murder, for it is impossible to be certain that he has no alibi. I decided instead that he must have a confederate within the household, and who more fitted for that part, my dear Miss Frayne, than you? You have access to Stephen at all times, you are the one person at Tarrington Chase known to be in sympathy with Hawkesworth, and you are even obliging enough to be in the habit of meeting him secretly." He laughed at her look of astonishment and dismay. "You thought no one knew that! You were with him yesterday at Meredith's house, and I dare say there have been other times, also."

Perdita moved carefully to the nearest chair and sat down. The situation had a nightmare quality, and she was mortally afraid, for she knew that Edward would not be talking so freely unless he intended to kill her, too. Her mind felt numb, stunned by the abrupt transition from excitement to horror, but she knew instinctively that she must encourage him to go on talking. As long as he did so, she was comparatively safe, and some chance of escape might offer itself.

"What motive am *I* supposed to have," she asked faintly, "for plotting Stephen's death?"

"Greed, Miss Frayne!" Edward's voice was mocking. "Hawkesworth is a rich man who keeps his mistresses in lavish style, and you have already taken the place of the Delamere woman. Who knows? As the price of murder he may even be prepared to marry you!"

Perdita closed her eyes for a moment. He could not possibly know that she was promised to Jason, yet she felt that that ugly suggestion of conspiracy and greed was somehow a desecration; that it sullied in some way the happiness they had found.

"It may console you to know, however," the hateful voice went on, "that though you, agreed to administer the laudanum which Hawkesworth provided, you found difficulty in bringing yourself to do the deed—until Lady Tarrington dismissed you. Then spite against her provoked you to it." He chuckled. "That was a stroke of good luck for me! I saw you slipping away yesterday and was curious enough to follow you, but I did not plan for her to discover your absence. I might have done so had it occurred to me, but it did not."

Perdita stole a glance at the clock on the mantelpiece and was amazed to see that barely a quarter of an hour had passed since her return to the schoolroom. The grotesque and horrible conversation seemed to have gone on for hours.

"Having committed the crime," Edward continued, "you are overcome by remorse, which not even the prospect of a life of luxury with Hawkesworth can conquer. You perceive, I trust, that I am painting your character as sympathetically as possible, and making him the real villain?" He paused inquiringly, but she could only stare at him with an incredulous horror which made him chuckle again. "Overcome, as I say, by remorse, you are going to take your own life, leaving behind a signed confession to all that I have just described. In the face of such evidence, none of Hawkesworth's denials will be believed."

"You are very ingenious, Mr Eastly!" Perdita thought she had found a flaw in his scheme, and that gave her the courage to reply. "But though you may be capable of killing me, and even of making it look like suicide, there is nothing you can do which will make me write such a confession."

"It is not necessary for you to write anything! I have the confession here!"

He put his hand into the breast of his coat and drew out a closely written sheet of paper. Unfolding it, he held it for Perdita to see, and the sense of nightmare unreality grew stronger, for the writing was her own.

"I flatter myself that this is an adequate replica of your hand," he said complacently, "and also that I have succeeded in capturing your style. It is my one really useful talent, Miss Frayne! I have found considerable profit in it during the past few years, though never, I must confess, of the kind it will bring me now. In the morning, this document will be found, and in view of all the other circumstances I feel tolerably certain that no one will question its authenticity."

He sounded triumphant, and Perdita knew with fearful certainty that he had good cause. If he could make it appear that she had taken her own life, the supposed confession would be accepted without question as the last testimony of a dying woman. Jason would guess the truth but he would have no hope of proving it, for in the hasty note she had sent him she had told him only that Edward was responsible for the murder attempts; she had not said why.

"Besides," Edward added after a brief pause, "the story is not entirely untrue, is it? Your intrigue with Hawkesworth is real enough! I suspected it when I saw him go to Meredith's while you were there, but that might have been a coincidence. So I offered you *my* help and protection, and when you refused it so scornfully, I was certain. No woman in your position could afford to be so improvident unless she was already well provided for." He paused, looking consideringly at her. "One has to admire your resourcefulness, you know! Your opportunities to capture Hawkesworth's fancy must have been very few, yet you seem to have found no difficulty in supplanting Miss Delamere. I am truly sorry that you are not to enjoy the full benefit of your success."

She looked at him with fear and loathing. "Spare me that, at least! If you feel no remorse for murdering a child, you are unlikely to feel it for anything less."

He smiled. "Perhaps not, but you must believe me when I tell you how grateful I am to you and Hawkesworth for making my task so easy. It was necessary for

Stephen to die—I shall not tell you for what reason—but I might have been suspected had no scapegoat been available. As it is, I shall be free to comfort Lady Tarrington in her bereavement, and I have every confidence that in time I shall come to fill Stephen's place in her affections."

As he spoke, he folded the paper and put it away. Then he took from his pocket the bell-rope he had cut.

"I devoted a good deal of thought to the manner of your suicide," he said conversationally as he uncoiled it, "and finally decided that you should hang yourself, One of the crossbeams in the corridor will serve the purpose admirably—though I fear that unfortunate servant-girl will have a severe shock in the morning."

He took a step towards her, and every other emotion —grief, anger, despair—was swallowed up by the blind, primitive instinct of self-preservation. She knew that she could not resist him physically, for though Edward was not a big man, he was stronger than he looked, as she had discovered when he dragged her into the schoolroom. She sprang forward in a frantic attempt to get past him and reach the door.

If she could have done so she would have stood a chance of escape, for once in the main part of the house it would be easy to raise the alarm; but he grabbed her as she tried to get past him, and she knew at once that she had no hope of breaking free. In a frenzy of terror she struck out with words where action was of no avail, and, perhaps because the thought had been uppermost in her mind only a little while ago, hit upon the one thing to say which he could not ignore.

"You will find no profit in murdering Stephen! Tarrington Chase belongs to Jason Hawkesworth!"

"What?" Edward's grip on her did not slacken, but now he was holding her before him and staring into her face. "What fairy-tale is that?"

"It is the truth!" Finding that she had caught his attention, she was able to speak less frantically. "Susan Hawkesworth was Sir Humphrey's lawful wife. He confessed it on his deathbed! Their son is Sir Jason Tarrington, the rightful heir!"

"You expect me to believe that?" Edward spoke with a sneer, but somehow his scorn lacked conviction. The tale was so preposterous that its very implausibility demanded consideration. "Even if it were true, how could you know it? You have only been in this house a few months!"

Briefly, still held before him in that painful grip, she told him, and saw uncertainty take the place of his former smug assurance. Pressing the advantage thus gained, she concluded:

"You need not take my word that it is so! Go to Lady Tarrington and challenge her about the secret she has kept for seven years, ever since Sir Humphrey died. Ask her why she hates Jason so bitterly, and why she persecuted his mother into suicide." She paused, and then with a flash of inspiration added the lie which might mean the difference between life and death. "And tell her the one thing she does not yet know! That the documents she sought so fruitlessly are already in Jason's possession! Nurse knew their hiding-place all along. She told me, and I had Gwenny take them to Dr Meredith's house on her way home this morning."

To her almost incredulous belief, she saw that her words had cast him into such uncertainty that he was no longer in command of the situation. He was ruthless and cunning, and as long as events moved along well-planned lines he would carry through his infamous schemes without faltering, but he lacked the ability to adapt those schemes without warning to altered circumstances. As clearly as though he had spoken them aloud, she recognised the doubts and fears which had now taken possession of him. For a few moments he continued to hold her, staring past her and gnawing at his lower lip, and then he flung her away from him so violently that she staggered half across the room and fetched up against the table with a force which made her cry out. Edward flung open the door.

"If you have lied to me, you vixen," he said savagely, "then, by God, I'll make you suffer for it!"

The door slammed behind him and the key grated in the lock. Perdita dragged herself painfully upright. She felt sick and shaken with the reaction from terror, but she knew she had gained only a temporary respite, unless she could escape from the schoolroom. The door was stout, but the lock might yield to a determined assault with the poker.

Suddenly she froze again in dismay, as the door handle was energetically rattled. She stared wordlessly at it, and then a voice she had thought never to hear again spoke urgently from beyond it.

"Miss Frayne! Miss Frayne, what is the matter? Why has Edward locked you in?"

"Stephen!" Her weakness forgotten, Perdita sprang across to the door, "Stephen, is that you?"

"Yes! Russet was growling, and that woke me up. When I looked out of my room Edward was locking this door. He seemed dreadfully angry."

Tears of thankfulness were pouring down Perdita's cheeks. It seemed like a miracle. Either Edward had lied about the laudanum, or . . . A sudden thought occurred to her.

"Stephen, did you drink your milk tonight?"

A prolonged and uncomfortable pause greeted the question, and then he said in a low, guilty voice: "No, ma'am. I tipped it out of the window as soon as you went out." Another pause, and then, with the air of one wishing to unburden his conscience completely: "I always do if I am left alone to drink it."

Perdita found that she was laughing as well as crying. With a tremendous effort she steadied her voice.

"Can you let me out?"

"No, ma'am! Edward took the key with him."

She thought quickly. "Stephen, listen to me, and do as I tell you immediately, without asking any questions. It is very, very important! Get dressed as quickly as you can, and go out by way of the spiral stair. Take Russet with you. Go down the Long Walk and across the meadow to the beginning of the path leading to Bryn Morgan's cottage. Mr Hawkesworth will be coming that way in a little while. Tell him what has happened to me, and then do exactly as he tells you. Do you understand?"

"Yes, Miss Frayne!" Stephen's voice was eager, vibrant with excitement. She could guess how much these extraordinary commands appealed to his sense of adventure. "Shall I go now?"

"Yes, and be sure to shut the door of your room when you go out, and the one into the garden. And, Stephen, if you hear Mr Eastly come back before you are ready, stay in your room and do not make a sound until he has come in here. Then go out as quietly as you can, no matter what else you may hear."

"Yes, Miss Frayne," he said again. "I'll be as quick as I can."

She heard the patter of his feet as he ran back to his room, and offered up a silent prayer that he would be able to accomplish his errand. It was only a little after half-past nine, but Jason might come early to the meeting-place. Meanwhile there was something she must do.

Following Nurse's instructions, she found and, after a struggle, succeeded in opening the secret hiding-place, and, groping within, drew out a bundle of papers tied with a thin silk cord. She untied it with trembling fingers, and a few moments later knew beyond doubt that everything the old woman had said was true. In that small packet was all the necessary proof that Jason was the legitimate son of Sir Humphrey Tarrington, and the rightful master of Tarrington Chase.

Slowly she did up the packet again, wondering what to do for the best. She could not guess what action Edward had taken after leaving the schoolroom, but if it occurred to him to question Nurse, he would inevitably discover that Perdita had lied when she said that the proof was already in Jason's possession. He might force Nurse to reveal where it had been hidden, therefore it would not do to replace it.

She tried to close the panel, but to her dismay this proved impossible. Either there was some trick to it which Nurse had neglected to tell her, or the ancient mechanism had finally ceased to function.

She picked up the papers and rose to her feet, looking anxiously about her. They must be hidden, for the significance of that gaping aperture in the panelling would be apparent to Edward the moment he entered the room.

On the wall facing her were two shelves of books, one belonging to Melissa, the other to Stephen. Perdita pulled forward some of the smaller volumes on Melissa's shelf, which was above eye-level, and dropped the packet down behind them, where it was completely hidden from view. It would not escape a really thorough search, but neither would any of the other hiding-places which suggested themselves.

The room was growing cold, for the fire which Bessie had made when she brought the milk had burned low, and Perdita, glad of any task, however trivial, to keep mind and hands occupied, busied herself with mending it. When that was done she sat beside it, watching the rising smoke and the little tongues of flame beginning to lick between the coals, until returning footsteps told her that the crisis was at hand.

She rose to meet it, standing erect and defiant in the light of the now brightening fire. The door opened, and to her astonishment and dismay, Lady Tarrington preceded Edward into the room. One look at them both told Perdita several things. It told her that Lady Tarrington was aware of the betrayal of her secret; that she was in one of her blind furies, but that for once it was under iron control and therefore even more to be feared; and that, whether Edward liked it or not, the leadership of the affair had passed from him to the old lady. She was there because she had chosen to come, and not through any persuasion of his.

Her ladyship was the first to see the gaping panel.

She looked at it for a moment and then turned to Perdita.

"So that is where the documents have been hidden," she said harshly, "and you lied when you said you sent them to Hawkesworth this morning! You have only just recovered them." To Edward she added curtly: "Hold her!"

He looked resentful, but apparently did not dare to disobey, and, coming up to Perdita, caught her wrists and jerked her arms roughly behind her back. She made one violent, unsuccessful effort to break free, and then stood passive, her cheeks scarlet with humiliation, while the old lady searched her.

"She has not hidden them upon her," Lady Tarrington announced at length, "so they must be somewhere in the room."

"I'll find them!" Edward said viciously, and jerked at Perdita's arms so that she gasped with pain. "Give me ten minutes, and she will be glad to tell where they are."

Lady Tarrington, confronting Perdita, saw defiance stronger than fear in the girl's eyes. She shook her head.

"A waste of time!" she said shortly. "It will be quicker to search the room." Her glance fell upon the bell-rope which he had dropped on the floor. She bent and picked it up, indicating one of the straight-backed chairs by the table. "Tie her to that! We will decide what to do with her once the papers have been found and burned."

He obeyed. Sullenly, resentfully, yet still—he obeyed, and that told Perdita more plainly than words

that whatever fate was marked out for after the papers
were found would be of Lady Tarrington's choosing.
The knowledge did nothing to reassure her. Of the two,
Edward would probably be the more merciful. She
stole a glance at the clock, and prayed that Jason
would come soon.

When Edward had bound her securely to the chair,
jerking the cord viciously tight, he pulled a handkerchief from his pocket and gagged her with it, saying
over his shoulder to Lady Tarrington:

"Better make sure she doesn't start screeching! It
would be awkward if the children were awakened."

Perdita shuddered at the callousness of the words,
since for all he knew, both Stephen and Melissa were
lying in a drugged sleep, the former, so Edward believed, never to wake again. She knew that his real
purpose was to prevent her from making any accusation against him, and bitterly regretted that she had not
done so as soon as Lady Tarrington entered the room.
She would not have been believed, but it might have
delayed for a little while the search for the documents,
and every moment saved would have increased the
chance of Jason arriving in time.

The old lady had simply nodded indifferently in answer to Edward, and had already begun to search the
room while he was making Perdita prisoner. She went
about the task with methodical efficiency, and Perdita
soon realised that there was no hope of the documents
being overlooked. She wondered what tale Edward had
told to account for his knowledge of them. Whatever it
was, it had obviously convinced her ladyship—or perhaps the only part of it which had impressed itself upon

her mind was the fact that her secret was known. Now she had been given the hope of keeping it, and also of destroying at last the only evidence of it. She seemed completely obsessed by the need to find and destroy the documents; every nerve and faculty was concentrated upon that one task. There was something weird and horrible about such single-mindedness, and Perdita shuddered again, knowing that once the documents had been destroyed, it would be turned with equal intensity to the task of silencing her.

Time passed. Edward, working his way along one side of the room while Lady Tarrington searched on the other, was examining the contents of the cupboard. It could be only a matter of minutes before he reached the bookshelves. Perdita cast another anguished glance at the clock, but the hands seemed scarcely to have moved.

She was beginning to feel faint. The fire had blazed up brilliantly, making the room warm again, and the gag knotted so tightly about her mouth made it difficult for her to breathe. She was cramped and aching from the tightness of her bonds, but her physical discomfort was nothing to her agony of mind.

Edward had almost completed his search of the cupboard; at any moment now he would start upon the bookshelves. The hands of the clock pointed at five to ten. Perdita, her head spinning, was engaged in frantic calculations. It would take Jason at least five minutes to reach the house from the edge of the woods; she had told Stephen to close the garden door, but it fastened only with an old-fashioned thumb-latch and could not be secured except by the massive bolts on the inside.

He would find no obstacle there. She knew that he would come—there was not the smallest doubt of that in her mind—but unless he came soon, his birthright would be lost to him for ever.

Edward turned to the bookshelves, pulling out each of Stephen's books in turn, and flicking through the pages before thrusting the volume back. In helpless anguish Perdita saw him turn his attention to the upper shelf, watched him treat Melissa's books the same way, heard his exclamation of triumph as the packet of papers was disclosed. He snatched it out, sending several of the books to the floor in his excitement.

"I have them!" he cried exultantly. "This is where the cunning little jade had hidden them!"

"Let me see!" Lady Tarrington had spun round at his first exclamation, and now came forward with hands outstretched like claws. "Give them to me!"

He did so, and she turned towards the table, where the light was strongest, tearing with trembling fingers at the cord. She unfolded the papers, and stared, her face livid and distorted, at the one which lay uppermost. It was the record of the marriage which had taken place between Humphrey Tarrington and Susan Hawkesworth in October, 1770, six months before her own "wedding".

"It is true!" she said in a harsh, terrible whisper. "Until this moment I never really believed it! Curse him! Curse them both!"

"Burn the papers!" Edward said urgently. "Burn them, ma'am, and then your secret will be safe!"

A sudden draught swept through the room, causing the fire to smoke and making the candle-flames flicker wildly. Jason's voice, quiet yet savagely mocking, spoke from the doorway.

"The secret, perhaps, whatever it may be," he said menacingly, "but I would not be willing to wager a groat, my friend, upon *your* immunity from danger!"

XIV

He was standing on the threshold, the height and breadth of him seeming to fill the ancient doorway, his black hair—for he was bareheaded—almost brushing the lintel. To two of the three occupants of the room there was something so uncanny about that sudden, silent arrival, in a house which they believed to be securely barred against all intruders, that they stood as though petrified in the attitudes in which his voice had surprised them. Shock held them motionless, more than the threat of the levelled pistol in his hand.

He moved forward a little, speaking a brief command, and Mahdu entered behind him and circled the room until he reached Perdita. He unfastened the gag, then drew a knife from the belt which girdled his tunic, and cut through the cord binding her hands. Jason, still watching Edward, asked quietly:

"Are you hurt, my dear?"

She moistened her dry lips, and spoke with some difficulty. "No, I am all right, but thank Heaven you came in time!"

He assumed this to mean that she had been in immediate physical danger, and the look which came into his eyes filled Edward with an alarm strong enough to restore the power of speech.

"In time to incriminate himself beyond all doubt!" he said viciously. "You see, Lady Tarrington, how bold they become? She must have left the garden door open for him—not for the first time, I'll wager! But we have him now! Not even that old fool, Redfall, can refuse to arrest a man who comes secretly, and armed, into another's house by night."

Jason, watching him with the utmost contempt, seemed unperturbed by the element of truth in Edward's words. If anyone came upon them now, the situation would appear utterly damning—the suspected man holding the mistress of Tarrington Chase at pistol point in her own house; but Jason knew that nothing short of an actual shot was likely to bring anyone else on the scene; and even if it had meant confronting every person in the house, he would still have come as soon as he heard of Perdita's plight.

Edward himself knew that there was little hope of making good his threat. Thanks to his own removal of the bell-rope, it was impossible to summon the servants, and though he carried a small pistol of his own, it availed him nothing while he was held at such a disadvantage. He glanced at Perdita. In a moment or two, when she had recovered a little from his rough handling of her, she would undoubtedly tell Hawkesworth the significance of the papers which Lady Tarrington was still clutching.

The same thought had already occurred to the old lady. From the moment of Jason's arrival she had not moved a muscle, merely staring at him with such concentrated malevolence that her thin, colourless face looked indescribably evil. She had always hated him as much as she had hated his mother, even from her own unassailable position as Sir Humphrey's wife. She had married a man she despised in order to acquire a title and to be the mistress of a great estate, and the achievement of that ambition had been her one constant consolation for six-and-thirty bitter years. Now she was to be deprived even of that. She had never been the wife of Humphrey Tarrington, and the son she had idolised had had no right to his father's name. By tomorrow that fact would be common knowledge. It was a humiliation she could not, would not face. With a movement so quick that it took even Jason by surprise, she turned and flung the bundle of documents unerringly into the blazing fire.

Perdita's reaction was the swiftest, and wholly instinctive. She saw the papers which meant so much to Jason on the point of being destroyed, and with a cry of dismay sprang from her chair and snatched them from the very heart of the fire. They were already alight, and she crushed them desperately between her hands, heedless—and, for the moment, totally oblivious —of the pain.

Lady Tarrington screamed once, a harsh, furious cry, and flung herself on the girl, striking and clawing with unnatural vigour in an attempt to secure possession of the papers. Jason started forward to restrain her, and Edward, who, the moment his attention was distracted by the old lady's first movement, had dragged out and cocked his own pistol, fired wildly after him.

One of the women uttered a gasping cry and they fell together to the floor in a confusion of struggling limbs, while Jason, pivoting on one foot, dealt Edward a terrific blow which sent him crashing into the corner amid the wreckage of a small table bearing Melissa's shell-work. He did not try to get up, and Jason, with a sick fear clutching at his heart, turned back to the two women.

Perdita was struggling to rise, and he gathered her into his arms and stood up. Her hair was coming down, the bodice of her dress had been ripped by the old lady's clawing hands and all the breath knocked out of her by the fall, but the shot had not touched her. As he held her tightly against him in a passion of thankfulness, Mahdu, rising from Lady Tarrington's side, said quietly:

"It is over, sahib! The old memsahib is dead!"

Jason felt Perdita shudder. He spoke quietly to Mahdu in his own tongue, and the servant bowed and went out of the room, while Jason laid Perdita on the sofa and sat down on the edge of it so that his body screened the old lady's huddled figure from her. She was still clutching the papers, and he took them gently from her, looking with angry concern at her burned and blistered hands. He would have put the documents aside without a glance, but she gasped urgently:

"Look at them, Jason! Was I quick enough? Are they still readable?"

He cast her a perplexed glance and unfolded the papers. They were charred now along their edges and stained with smoke, but still perfectly legible, and for a long moment he stared at the marriage certificate as though he could not believe what he saw. Then he passed slowly to the next document, and the next, while Perdita, watching his face, counted the agony of her burned hands a small price to pay for the look she saw there.

Mahdu returned with a blanket which he had taken from Stephen's bed. He spread it over Lady Tarrington's body, and then turned to Jason.

"They come, sahib!" he said placidly. "That shot roused the household."

Jason looked at him for a second or two as though he did not see him, and then the significance of the words pierced his preoccupation. He rose, picked up the pistol which he had laid on the table, and returned to stand by the sofa. He spoke a low-voiced command, and Mahdu heaved Edward up into a chair and stationed himself beside him. Eastly was beginning to come round, but was still not fully aware of what was happening.

The door was flung open by a footman, who halted abruptly to stare at the scene confronting him, while his companions crowded close behind, trying to see what had caused his dismay. Jason, still holding the pistol, though he made no move to level it, said curtly:

"I want to see the most senior among you. Fetch them to me at once!"

They were too startled, or too nonplussed, to disobey, or perhaps they felt the need for someone more responsible to take the initiative. Whatever the reason, one of them hurried away, while the others still crowded in the doorway, staring uneasily at Edward, slumped in his chair, and at the still shape beneath the blanket. Eventually approaching footsteps were heard, and they drew back to make way for Mrs Price, Mervyn, the butler, and Lady Tarrington's maid. Jason stepped forward to the table and spread the documents out before the newcomers.

"Read those!" he commanded briefly. "Your mistress is dead, shot by Edward Eastly, but those papers will assure you of *my* right to give orders here."

Puzzled and suspicious, but overawed by his manner, they did as he told them. It took several minutes for the meaning of what they read to dawn upon them, but at last Mrs Price raised a white, shocked face.

"Did her ladyship know this, sir?"

"She knew of the existence of those documents, but until tonight she had never seen them," he replied shortly. "Are you the housekeeper?" She assented, and he went on: "Be good enough to help Miss Frayne to bed. She has suffered a severe shock, and her hands are badly burned. I will have Dr Meredith sent for immediately."

He turned to Perdita and helped her to her feet. She made no protest, for she had almost reached the end of her endurance, and only said anxiously: "Stephen?"

"With Bryn, at the cottage. I will send Mahdu to

fetch him." He stood for a moment, holding her lightly
by the arms, and then, careless of the watching servants, bent and kissed her. "Go to bed, my love! There
is nothing more to fear." To the startled Mrs Price he
added: "Prepare one of the guest chambers for her.
After what has happened tonight, I do not want her to
stay in this part of the house."

"Yes, sir!" Mrs Price seemed too shaken to do any
thing but obey. "What about Miss Melissa, sir? The
noise must have wakened her."

With a tremendous effort, Perdita summoned enough
strength to explain how Edward had admitted drugging
the children's milk. She knew this must be told, though
she was too dazed with pain and weariness to know
what reaction it aroused in her hearers, or whether Edward himself tried to deny it.

After that she was vaguely aware of Mrs Price helping her to bed, and later of Owen Meredith dressing
her burned hands and making her swallow some kind of
medicine. After that she slept, woke briefly in grey
morning light, and slept again.

In the afternoon she roused more fully, to surroundings which puzzled her by their unaccustomed luxury,
until the soreness of her bandaged hands recalled the
events of the previous night. At once anxiety took possession of her, for her memory of what had happened
after Lady Tarrington's death was muddled and hazy.
Jason had seemed to be in complete command of the
situation then, but had he remained so after the servants recovered from their first shock?

It was fortunate for her peace of mind that Dr
Meredith arrived to see her before she had been awake

for more than half an hour. Attended by Mrs Price, he
came to stand by the bed, looking down at his patient
with kind, perceptive eyes.

"So you are awake, my dear young lady," he remarked, "and unless I am much mistaken, have been
fretting yourself into a sad state of nerves for no reason
at all."

"Is there no reason, sir?" she asked anxiously. "Pray
tell me the truth! Nothing could be worse than what I
have been imagining."

"There is no reason in the world," he assured her,
preparing to examine her hands. "Last night Jason sent
at once for Sir Charles Redfall. When Sir Charles
questioned Eastly, the young scoundrel broke down
and confessed everything. Lady Tarrington wanted to
provide for him, but Sir Humphrey had tied up the estate so securely that she could touch no part of it.
Eastly persuaded her to promise that he should marry
Melissa as soon as she was old enough, and planned to
kill Stephen so that his sister would inherit everything.
The old lady's hatred of Jason, and Jason's own attitude, provided him with a convenient scapegoat."

Perdita shuddered. "How could he be so heartless!
Stephen liked and trusted him, and he knew that the
child meant more to Lady Tarrington than anything in
the world."

"Edward Eastly is incapable of caring for anyone
but himself," Owen replied grimly, unwinding one of
the bandages. "Yes, that is very satisfactory, though I
fear you will find those burns painful for some time.
You are a very courageous and very reckless young

woman, you know! You could easily have been very seriously injured, or even killed, had your clothing chanced to catch fire."

"I had to save those documents," Perdita replied simply. "Dr Meredith, what has happened to the children?"

"Lady Redfall came this morning and took them to stay with her. It was essential for them to be removed from this house without delay."

"Do they know what has happened?"

"They have been told that their grandmother is dead, but that is all. The rest will have to be explained to them later—and I give thanks that it will not fall to my lot to do it"

"Yes, indeed!" she agreed in a low voice. "Oh, poor children! If only they could have been spared!"

"The innocent are usually the victims," Owen said gravely. "Do not forget how bitterly Jason and his mother suffered for many years. Humphrey Tarrington was a coward and a fool! He could have sealed up those documents and left them with his lawyer, to be opened only after his death, but he trusted no one. Men such as he often wreak as much harm as rogues like Eastly."

Perdita recognised the truth of this, but it could not lessen her distress on the children's behalf, which was so great that she was scarcely aware of the painful process of having her hands dressed again. Her hurts would heal; would Stephen and Melissa ever recover from theirs?

Owen completed his task and then stood looking thoughtfully down at her.

"You will stay where you are, Miss Frayne, for the next few days," he said with some decision. "Sir Charles wants to question you, but he will wait until *I* consider you are strong enough. Jason has made that very clear to him." He saw that she still looked troubled, and patted her shoulder reassuringly. "There is nothing more for you to be uneasy about, my dear! I give you my word on that!"

She tried to believe him, but could not rid herself of a lingering doubt. What was happening elsewhere in the great house? How was Jason faring, in the first, uneasy hours of his inheritance?

Darkness had fallen. The curtains of crimson brocade had been drawn across the windows, and firelight and candlelight filled the handsome room with their comfortable glow. Perdita, propped against a heap of downy pillows, was wishing wretchedly that Dr Meredith had seen fit to give her another dose of the sleeping-draught which had proved so effective the night before.

Mrs Price's agitated voice became audible outside the door. The words were indistinguishable, but the tone of shocked disapproval was eloquent enough without them. Jason's impatient voice answered her, and then he walked into the room, shutting the door firmly in the housekeeper's outraged face.

Perdita gasped. She could not wonder that Mrs Price was shocked, for this was unheard of, and not even a betrothal was sufficient excuse for a visit of this kind.

Her heart might leap with delight at sight of him, and the troubled world be miraculously set to rights, but the first words she spoke had to be of reproof.

"Oh, you should not be here! Or, at least, Mrs Price ought to be present!"

He came to the bedside, looking down at her without the least sign of repentance. "Did you suppose I could do without a sight of you until Owen sees fit to let you get up? Or that I want a servant, all eyes and ears, in the background? You know I have no regard whatsoever for propriety."

Perdita was beginning to think that she had none, either, for even as she reproached him she had held out her bandaged hands in a gesture of welcome. He took them very gently in his, the jesting look fading from his eyes.

"If I could have spared you this!" he said in a low voice. "My little love, I wish you had not done it!"

"My hands will soon heal," she replied, "but I would never have forgiven myself if those documents had been burned. The truth *had* to be made known!" She looked anxiously at him. "It will, will it not? There is sufficient proof?"

"There is more than enough!" Jason, still holding her hands, sat down on the edge of the bed. "Redfall confirms that, though there will be a great many damnably tedious legal formalities to be gone through before everything is settled. Meanwhile, he informs me, I am to take charge here, since the estate cannot be left in the hands of servants. I imagine he feels that since I have been spared my proper responsibilities for so long, I cannot now assume them quickly enough."

He spoke lightly, but with an underlying bitterness which she was quick to detect.

"You are thinking, are you not, that the truth ought to have been made known during your mother's lifetime?" she said gently. "And that if you had been in Tarrington when Sir Humphrey died, it might have been?"

"Is it not so?" The bitterness in his voice was undisguised now. "Oh, I do not blame the old lady for concealing it! She had been as greatly wronged as anyone, and she was fighting for her own. But if I had been here, and had known the truth, my mother might be alive today!" He was not looking at Perdita now, but past her into the shadows, and his dark face wore its most predatory and ruthless look. "God knows I always hated my father, but never so much as when I learned the truth last night!"

"Yet your mother loved him, Jason," Perdita reminded him. She spoke hesitantly, for though her heart ached to comfort him, she feared that she was intruding where she had no right to be. "It was not for her own sake that she wanted the truth made known, but for yours. For her sake, can you not try to forgive him?"

Slowly his gaze came back to her face, softening a little as it met her anxious, loving look. "A forgiving nature, my love, has never been among my few virtues, but there is truth in what you say. Perhaps in time I may be able to think less hardly of him." He was silent for a moment, and then added abruptly: "I do not yet know the extent of the fortune the old lady brought here as her dower, but whatever it was, that amount shall be put in trust for Stephen and Melissa. The Tarringtons have no shadow of right to it, and those unfortunate children must be provided for."

Perdita freed one hand from his and touched his cheek lightly with her fingertips. Her eyes were very bright. "Not a forgiving nature, perhaps," she said softly, "but a very generous one. I am glad you mean to do that."

"Conscience money, it will be said," he retorted with a grin. "I do not feel particularly generous. Just damnably impatient!" He lifted the hand he still held, and, pushing back her sleeve, dropped a kiss on the inside of her wrist. "I meant to marry you in two days' time, and now, with all these confounded complications, and Eastly's trial, devil knows how long we may have to wait!"

"Perhaps," she said slowly, her eyes clouding, "we ought not to marry at all."

"Ought not . . . ?" He looked searchingly at her, and then grinned again. "Are you endeavouring to cry off, Miss Frayne?"

She raised troubled eyes to his. "I mean it, Jason! It might have been permissible for Mr Hawkesworth to marry a mere governess, but for Sir Jason Tarrington . . ."

He leaned forward and kissed her, giving her no chance to complete the sentence. Then, having silenced her protest, said calmly:

"Sir Jason Tarrington, my foolish one, will do exactly as Jason Hawkesworth has always done—live his life as he pleases, and not as the world may think he should. I'll wager you have no more desire than I have to rule the roost in Tarrington, but, as Redfall points out, one cannot have the advantages without the responsibilities. At least I now have a name to offer you! It's not one in which it is possible to take much pride, but I'm damned if I'll allow you to jilt me on that account!"

"I did not mean that!" she said indignantly. "You know I did not!"

"I know very well what you meant, and a confounded absurdity it is. I want to hear no more of it!" He paused, meeting her still troubled, doubtful gaze with an amused look. "You have no choice, you know! I am completely unscrupulous as well as lacking any regard for propriety, and you are now so thoroughly compromised that you will have to marry me. I warned you the other day that I did not mean you to escape."

She recalled the glimpse she had had of Mrs Price's outraged expression as Jason came into the room, and knew that as far as Tarrington was concerned, he was not exaggerating. The prim Miss Frayne ought to have been horrified. Perdita simply gave a little gasp of laughter, and abandoned an argument which she had no desire to win.